GROUNDED AT GROOM LAKE

D1635053

GROUNDED AT GROOM LAKE

JEFF NORTON.com

Marianne!

Happy World Book Day!

AWESOME READS

March 7 2019

First published in 2018 by Awesome Reads

Copyright © Awesome Media & Entertainment Ltd., 2018
With special thanks to Matt Knight

The moral right of Jeff Norton to be identified as the
author of this work has been asserted in accordance with
the Copyright, Designs and Patents Act 1988.

All rights reserved. No part of this publication may be
reproduced or transmitted in any form or by any means,
electronic or mechanical including photocopying, recording
or any information storage or retrieval system, without
prior permission in writing from the publishers.

This novel is entirely a work of fiction. The names,
characters and incidents portrayed in it are the work of the
author's imagination.
Any resemblance to actual persons, living or dead, events
or localities is entirely coincidental.

ISBN 978-1-911195-96-2

Also available as an ebook
ISBN 978-1-911195-97-9

Designed & typeset by K.DESIGN, Winscombe, Somerset
Cover design by Margaret Hope
Printed and bound by Clays Ltd, Elcograf S.p.A.

"This is Sherman's story, and it's printed in American
spelling and grammar to most accurately reflect his voice.
If you're reading this outside of the United States, we hope
you don't mind the funny spelling."

For Caden – shoot for the stars.

Check out these other Awesome books

If you want a good laugh . . .

MEMOIRS OF A NEUROTIC ZOMBIE

Published by Faber & Faber

If you want a thrilling adventure . . .

METAWARS

Published by Orchard Books

If you want a rock'n'roll whodunit . . .

KEEPING THE BEAT

Published by KCP Loft

All this and *more* at **www.jeffnorton.com**

Contents

Prologue

I placed the urn gently into the rocket, holding Mom's remains for the very last time. "You're finally going to get your wings," I whispered as I closed the metal hatch.

The rocket was twice as tall as me, assembled from spare parts I'd scrounged from around the base. I'd spent the last eight months planning this launch and calculated that the rocket would hit sixty thousand feet, the edge of space, in four minutes and thirty-two seconds. I was determined to grant Mom the one thing in death she always dreamed of in life, but never achieved: her astronaut wings.

I'd considered inviting Dad and Jessica to the launch, but I knew they just wouldn't understand. This was between Mom and me.

You see, rockets were *our* thing; our shared love. She always encouraged me to pursue rocketeering, no doubt channeling her own unfulfilled space dreams. So, while most of the people at the US Air Force base in Geilenkirchen were watching my twin sister Jess belt out musical numbers in the school play, I kneeled down in the base's scrapyard beside my most ambitious rocket yet and lit the fuse.

Ten. . .nine. . .eight. . .seven. . .six. . .five. . .four. . .three . . . two . . .

"Goodbye, Mom."

. . . one.

The rocket lit up the night sky, taking my mother to the heavens. It was a perfect launch and a perfect tribute – exactly one year since her death.

And that's when I heard the sirens.

CHAPTER ONE

Arrival

You'd think that, after ten years of institutional education, at seven different schools in seven different countries, I'd be used to the first day of school by now. But no matter what base Dad got stationed to, I was always the outsider: getting picked last in gym class, living in the shadow of Jess's overactive social life and eating whatever passed for food in the host country, by myself, in a cafeteria filled with people who just weren't as smart as Sherman Capote.

On our first Nevada morning, Jess and I walked in silence along the perfectly paved asphalt, past beige office buildings and beige Air Force standard-issue bungalows with manicured lawns, minutes away from joining another mid-term Newcomers' Club. I looked up and noticed wispy clouds hanging in the dawn sky over the Groom Lake desert, our newest home.

Noctilucent clouds – the highest kind of clouds you could get.

Right at the edge of space.

Well, there's no actual *edge* – of space – the molecules of air just get further and further apart – but that's where a man called Theodore von Kármán drew a line between Earth's atmosphere and the rest of the solar system. Up there, where there's hardly any air and barely any gravity, a rocket has what's called Six Degrees of Freedom.

6DoF.

Six degrees of freedom.

Freedom. That's what I wanted as I marched towards another new school I wouldn't fit into. What I'd got, however, was a military arrest, a midnight airlift and a forced relocation back to the States for the fractured Capote family.

"Do you hear that, Sherman?" Jessica asked, breaking the silence.

"What, you talking?"

"Ha ha," she said. "Very *not* funny. No, insects."

Now that she mentioned it, I could hear rhythmic chirruping like in the background of movie campfire scenes.

"I think they're called cicadas," I said.

"And do you know why we can hear *sick*-addas?" Jessica droned on.

I did, actually. "It's an integral part of their mating ritual – the male makes the song to attract the female across the desert and—"

She punched me on the arm. Hard. Now don't be fooled. Jess might look like a malnourished goth queen, but she punches like a heavyweight. And before you worry, she eats just fine.

"We can hear them because we *live* in the desert now," she said. "With the insects!"

"Can't you just drop it?"

"Are you *ever* gonna tell me why you did it, Sherm? I mean, you sneak off and fire a missile—"

"It was a rocket," I corrected her.

"From an Air Force base," she continued. "Where rockets go by their maiden name: *missiles*."

"I'm sorry," I lied. "I've said I'm sorry a thousand times. I said it to Dad. I said it to the Joint Chiefs. I said it to the Russian President on the phone, *Mne zhal*, which is actually really hard to say, but if you want it one more time, okay, Jess – I'm . . . *sorry*."

But I wasn't. And I never would be.

"You almost completed the World War trilogy, Sherman!"

Of course, I'd had no intention of starting a war.

I'm actually a pacifist at heart – more of a lover than a fighter. Okay, I'm not really a lover or a fighter, but on the fourth of March, one year after Mom's death, I had reasons for my space-bound tribute. *Reasons* it had to be a rocket. Reasons it had to fly *that* high. But they were *my* reasons. And the one good thing – the *only* good thing – about finally arriving at our new school, was that it got Jessica off the subject.

Our mom, Carol Capote, always wanted to go into space. She was only three years old when Neil Armstrong took one small step for man. Unfortunately, Neil didn't say anything about man *and* woman. As she watched the black and white moonwalk from Grandpa's lap, Mom declared that she was going to be an astronaut too. But in those days, the closest a *girl* could ever get to outer space was serving drinks at twenty-five thousand feet on a 707. Gran and Grandpa discouraged Mom from anything astronautical and nudged her into nursing.

But she stayed adventurous.

She chose nursing in the US Army Medical Service Corps, and then during Desert Storm she met Dad, and one thing led to another, and that *another*, I suppose, led to Jess and me. So, had she done what she'd really wanted to do with her life, neither of us would exist.

That was the thought knocking around in my head as Jess and I arrived at the beige, three-storey concrete block soon to be known as our new school. Its darkly tinted, rectangular windows glinted in the morning sun, and the immaculate front lawn soaked up the water from a row of tiny, twirling sprinklers. The schoolyard was empty. Not a single student or teacher in sight.

"It's freakily quiet around here," Jessica said. "Kinda like a Sherman Capote birthday party."

"It's nice and quiet when you're not talking," I said.

We headed up the concrete steps to the glass doors under the silver letters that spelled out: GROOM LAKE HIGH SCHOOL.

★ ★ ★

The long central hallway was empty, populated only by trophy cabinets and plaques, and the shiny, checkered floor smelled of polish and disinfectant.

"You must be the new . . . " called a voice. We turned round to see a hairless man with bleach-white skin in a dark suit. His bald head was dominated by thick, black-rimmed glasses and his eyes – devoid of color, like two fried eggs with black yolks – widened when he saw our faces. "Kids?" he finished.

If you look closely at school principals all over the

world, in the corner of their mouths they're quietly counting. Counting the hours until the school day finishes, counting the days until summer vacation, and counting the years until retirement will save them from schoolyard skirmishes, breakdown-inducing field trips, and confrontational parent-teacher nights. Having experienced seven schools in ten years, I had a finely-tuned radar for mouth-counting. And this albino administrator was counting the seconds.

"I'm Sherman Capote and this is Jessica. And sadly, we are related."

"This is most unusual," he said. "Where did you come from?"

"I know, right?" Jess sighed. "How can we come from the same gene pool?"

"We landed last night," I said. "Our dad, General Frank Capote, told us to show up for school early."

"I see. Well, I'm Principal Meltzer," he said. I took another long look. He really was hairless. Nothing at all – no eyebrows, no eyelashes, not even a patch of protruding nasal hair. "Come into my office, I think there's been a mix-up. This isn't really a school for your, um, type."

"Geeks?" asked Jessica, tilting her head towards me.

"Drama queens?" I suggested, nodding at her.

Meltzer led us into his office, which was ridiculously tidy and exactly the kind of place you'd expect – filing cabinets, desk, computer, window overlooking the front lawn – except, for some reason, it was all just a little bit *slicker* than any other school office I'd been in. The cabinets were reflective chrome with flashy digital locks. The desk seemed to hover in the air and the computer was *insanely* thin, thinner than anything I'd ever seen. And I never miss an Apple keynote.

Meltzer got busy adjusting his thick glasses, checking his email and calling his secretary. It seemed we were just one issue of hundreds that needed sorting before the morning bell even rang.

"Don't get me wrong," he said to us, "I'm pro-diversity, but to start *this* school without a security overview *or* an induction briefing—"

"But, sir," I said, "apparently we're under orders to report here."

"If you were under orders," Meltzer said, "you'd have had your security overview and your induction briefing."

"We just landed," I said.

"Under armed guard," Jessica moaned. "But we could just go home if you—"

"Capote, you say?" Meltzer asked, squinting his white

eyes at his computer screen. "Here it is. *Holy permission slip*, you minnows are already enrolled by the highest level." He turned back to us with a disappointed look. "Why do the military have to be so, so . . . *militarized* about everything?"

"So we're in the right place?" I asked.

"I wouldn't go that far," Meltzer replied. "But you're my problem now. So go have your vaccinations – and welcome to the next chapter in your academic career."

Outside, way overhead, a jet flew by. The distant roar of it filled the office while Meltzer's words sank in.

"Why do we need vaccinations?" I asked.

"This place is an overflowing Petri dish of foreign bugs. Everyone gets the injection. Nurse Anderson's office is around the corner," he said, waving us away. "Oh, and try not to get eaten. That just means more paperwork."

"Eaten?" asked Jess.

"Figure of speech," I said, hopefully. "Little minnows, big pond?"

"Yeah, that's it," said Meltzer. "But steer clear of a pupil named Graz."

"Who?" asked Jess.

"Huge hairy fella, doesn't take well to newcomers. I'd call him a bully, but that's giving bullies a bad name."

The phone *beep-beeped* and Meltzer waggled his hand at us towards the door as he grabbed the receiver.

"Oh . . ." Jessica groaned, swinging her black hair over her shoulder, "how I *hate* you, Sherman Capote."

★ ★ ★

We left the office and walked through a set of glass doors in the hallway. I took a moment to look at myself in the reflection: my disheveled bedhead hair (well, technically airplane-head hair), peach-fuzz face and red hoodie; the displaced Capote kid. The guy who almost started World War Three. I tried to smile, to stay on the bright side (war had been averted!), but a crooked, resigned grimace was all that smirked back at me.

I thought back to my last first day of school, in Germany, almost two years ago. Mom made her perfectly burned French toast (our first-day-of-school ritual) and served it with freshly-squeezed orange juice and side of pep-talk.

"Sherman, I know it's hard starting new schools," she'd said, even though I'm not sure that she did know, "but you are a special, smart, sensitive boy and you're going to be spectacular."

She always used "*s*" words with me. Jessica got complimentary adjectives too, but never beginning with "*j*". Alliteration, like rockets, was just for me and Mom.

This was the first *first* day I'd have without her – the first of many firsts I'd have without her. I was in the middle of the desert with my twin sister who hated me, my dad who would barely talk to me and a school that clearly didn't want me.

I felt unimaginably alone in the universe.

CHAPTER TWO

Bully Allergies

If my math is right – and it usually is – I've spent ninety-nine-point-four per cent of my fourteen years on Planet Earth away from the US, following Dad from one Air Force base to another: South Korea (it's not all Gangnam style; they care about your *kibun* there, very cool), France (strange food, population no ruder than anywhere else), England (can't go wrong with fish and chips, but cars driving on the wrong side of the road made crossing the street dangerous) and most recently Germany (weird toilets and scene of my rocketry "incident").

And so far, it's true. *Everything* is bigger back in the States.

The Groom Lake High nurse's office wasn't an office. It was a basketball-court-sized, gleaming-white sick bay; all dazzling strip-lights and funky hydraulic gurneys and rows of (really *tall*) curtained cubicles.

"This place is immense," I said.

"To treat bully victims," teased Jessica. "You heard what Meltzer said!"

We wandered towards the office space at the back (more chrome cabinets and slick computers), eyeballing each cubicle as we went. Every curtain was open and every cubicle empty except the last one, which had its curtain drawn. I was wondering who was in there when suddenly the world shook.

"*AAAAAAACHOO.*"

It wasn't a sneeze.

It was Sneeze-zilla.

Sneeze-point-eight on the Richter scale.

The kind of sneeze that could burst only from someone so staggeringly, alarmingly huge that it *had* to be Graz.

The curtain swished open – my heart leaped into my mouth for a second – but what emerged was just a bright-eyed, normal-sized nurse. She pulled the curtain closed behind her, then beamed at us.

"So you're the new kids I just got emailed about?"

Jessica and I nodded, glancing over her shoulder at the twitching curtain.

"I guess Meltzer's finally taking that diversity policy seriously," the nurse said. "So, welcome to Groom

Lake! I'm Nurse Anderson. And you're here for the dreaded—"

She stuck out her lower lip and motioned injecting herself in her arm.

We nodded again. Glanced again.

"Piece of cake, sweetie pies," she said. "Pick a bay each and I'll be right back with the drugs. Say, it's too *quiet* in here."

She shimmied behind the desk, tapped the computer screen and immediately the place bounced with boxy-sounding drums, a jangly guitar and Nurse Anderson belting out Motown music.

I chose the open cubicle next to the übersneezer's, and Jessica sat in the one opposite.

"Hey, Jess," I said as I jumped on the white-sheeted bed. "Did you see her brooch?"

"Yes, I saw it," Jessica said, "and I don't want to talk about it."

"Same as Mom's," I said.

The silver badge was called a Caduceus. The two snakes entwined around a winged staff were the insignia of the US Medical Corps. When Mom died, the army sent a brooch just like it back from Afghanistan (along with the rest of her "personal effects"). It's what gave me the idea.

For the rocket.

For sending Mom past the Kármán Line.

Because if you fly that high, the military gives you your astronaut badge.

Your wings.

I wanted Mom to get her wings.

"What are you in for?" asked the deepest voice I'd ever heard, rumbling from Sneeze-zilla's cubicle. Jessica and I just stared at each other for a moment – mouths open, no doubt looking dopey – until, finally, she mouthed, *Answer him.*

"Vaccinations," I said. "How about you?"

"Allergy shots," he said in grave, bass tones. Wow, this guy sounded *ill*.

"Do you have bad allergies?" I asked, attempting a hey-everything-is-cool voice. But it came out more like I was taking his coffee order.

"Rained last night," he gurgled. "Figured I'd be safe in the desert. Hah!"

Jessica's eyes widened and she pointed at the curtain.

Graz . . . ? she mouthed. She smiled and smacked her fist into her palm.

My sister took an unhealthy delight in seeing her twin brother being picked on at new schools, and she was clearly looking forward to the next round.

"Quit your whining, big fella," the nurse called from the office. "You'll be fine once that shot kicks in."

"Never lasts long enough," he complained.

"That's what the special cream is for," she said.

"I have an acute sister allergy," I said, hoping that some banter might make me less of a bully target. "Do they have cream for that?"

He laughed so hard it shook the floor and I figured it was safe to introduce myself.

"My name's Sherman," I said. "What's yours?"

Please not Graz, please not Graz, please not Graz ...

"Unless you're from my depth of the sea," the voice growled, "it's impossible to pronounce. Kids round here lack imagination, so they just call me Octo."

Octo.

Okay, so, weird voice, weird sense of humor and weird name. But at least he wasn't the bully I'd been warned about, which pretty much made him my new best friend. I would have offered to shake his allergy-ridden hand, but Nurse Anderson swished round the corner, holding a syringe the size of a bazooka.

CHAPTER THREE

Breakfast Club

We were back in the hallway – more lockers and trophy cabinets and posters for club meetings – outside the brushed-aluminium double doors to the cafeteria.

"I can't believe you want to eat," Jessica said, massaging her arm, "after *that*."

"I didn't have any breakfast, and I could use a cream soda to settle my stomach," I said. "And you passed out. So *you* need to eat something too."

"Promise me you won't do anything to get us kicked out of another school."

"I promise," I said, crossing my fingers behind my back. On the other side of the doors, I could hear plates being stacked and clinking cutlery and kids – a *lot* of kids – probably the entire Groom Lake student body.

A whole new school not to fit into.

"Time to meet the locals," I said, placing a hand on

the cool door. Jess straightened herself and put on a bright stage-smile.

I pushed open the doors and stopped dead. Had the injection reached my brain and started vandalizing it?

I was seeing things. Strange things.

And when I say *things*, what I really mean is *creatures*.

The cafeteria was crowded with creatures. The entire room, dotted with two dozen hexagonal lunch tables, was heaving with creatures – furry, slimy, bendy, floral and robotic.

Talking mushrooms clung onto the walls alongside the club posters and football pennants. These beach-ball-sized brown fungi, with beady eyes and skinny little arms, were yelling at each other in squeaky voices.

"Listen, Zero-Charisma – you can't just be fungi, you gotta be a FUN GUY, you know?!"

They also seemed to be shouting at some shy-looking slug-things who were hunched around a hexagonal table and rolling their eyes – their eyes on *stalks* – and ignoring them.

"Hey, slimer! Aww, why the sad face? Ooh, wait. I get it. You ain't a slug, you're a snail with a housing problem – I'm right, right?!"

The obnoxious mushrooms were also teasing some weird, bendy cylinders that rippled around another table like the blow-up figures you see outside used-car dealerships.

"Hey, airhead! Body-poppin's on its way out. Get some fresh moves, bro!"

They were even yelling at an NBA-tall, tank-wide yeti monster in the corner. A guy with burning tiger-eyes and razor-sharp fangs.

"Hey, fuzzball! You've only chomped seventy-eight eyeburgers, dude! How yer gonna last till lunch?!"

I heard some sniggers and looked to my left. A tableful of little gray guys, with big black eyes on bulbous heads on top of toddler-sized bodies clothed in zip-up silver jumpsuits, were giggling and pointing at us. I managed a glare, and they went back to trading food between them.

Straight ahead, a table of industrial-looking black-and-yellow robots, like bipedal diggers, took a break from blasting techno tunes from little round speakers in their chests to shake their heads at us.

To our right, black, potted flowers in ninja-warrior poses – their pots slotted into circular holes in their chairs – rolled their leafy eyes at us, then ignored us completely.

Jessica gripped my arm. My *very sore* arm.

"Sherman!" she yelped. "What *is* this?"

"You see it too?" I asked, blinking. I suppose we did get the same injections.

"Are we crazy?" she said.

At this point, I was wondering that myself. "I think maybe Nurse Anderson gave us the wrong kind of injection," I whispered.

But just then I spotted one lone human amid the sea of creatures. I grabbed Jess and led her to the food counter. A plump, bespectacled, and most importantly, *normal-looking* lady stood behind the counter. She was holding a ladle and sized us up like we were going to shoplift.

"Is all this, like . . . " Jessica began, "um, like, some kinda theme park or something?"

The lunch lady – her red hair jammed into a net, her four-leaf-clover tattoo rippling on her forearm – winked at Jessica and laughed. "Hon, it's not so much a theme park here, darlin', but a *circus*."

"So . . . " my sister hissed, grinding her teeth a little, "does that mean 'yes' or—"

"How 'bout we keep it movin' here, honey," said the lunch lady, whose nametag read *Nancy*. "What'll it be? *Local . . . ?*"

She flicked a switch on the gleaming counter, and half the lids buzzed open to show rows and rows of fried eggs, streaky bacon, bagels, waffles and even French toast.

It smelled great. My stomach rumbled in anticipation. We'd landed from our airlift just after four a.m., then had long enough to catch a low-wattage power nap before Dad woke us up and shoved us out of our new home – a very beige Air Force bungalow – to report for school. I hadn't had time for breakfast and was yearning for the most important meal of the day.

". . . or *Universal* ?" she asked, and this time the rest of the lids slid open to reveal rows of gelatinous, pulsating somethings I never, ever wanted to see again.

The spread smelled like well-aged sushi. My stomach turned and I was suddenly glad that I'd skipped breakfast. There was nothing down there to bring up.

"Is that supposed to be *food*?" Jessica gasped, holding her nose.

My stomach fought a civil war between hunger and disgust. As long as I looked away from the "Universal" offerings, hunger was winning. "I'd like some French toast please, Nancy," I said, determined to take this chance to fill up. "Medium-well done."

"Sherman, are you deranged?" Jessica snapped. "We're going back to the nurse. We need medical attention."

"But if I don't eat something first," I said, "I'm gonna keel over."

"Where's your tray?" Nancy snapped.

"Oh," I said, "er—"

She grabbed a clear plastic tray from under the counter, then passed me an amateurishly-charred but otherwise tasty-looking plateful of French toast.

"And for you?" she asked Jessica. "You look like you could do with some fattening up."

"Why? So those things out there can eat me?"

"Come on, Jess," I urged. "You can't survive on sarcasm alone."

"Fine, keep it moving," Nancy said, and then looked up – and up. "What do you want, young man? Haven't you had enough already?"

I could swear she was talking to the ceiling tiles.

"YOU, TINY NEW KID," boomed a voice behind me. "YOU GONNA EAT THAT?"

So Octo the Allergy Boy didn't have the deepest voice in the universe after all. It was actually kind of shrill compared to the dinosaur-chewing-boulders voice coming from above and behind me.

"I SAID, 'ARE YOU GONNA EAT THAT?'"

There didn't seem much else to do except – very, very slowly – turn around. So we did. And it was something about the *stink* of the grayish-black wall of fur we came face-to-knee with that told me that this was really happening; that this whole cafeteria wasn't a figment of my imagination. I couldn't dream up a smell this bad. He smelled like my dead dog's butt.

We had to put Goose down a few years ago because of an intestinal thing. I still miss him, but, man, I don't miss those farts.

The mushrooms started chanting in our direction.

"Gimme a 'G' . . . "

I suppose the sensible thing would've been to run, but instead I just froze, gazing up at the shaggy face with the tiger eyes and the obscenely fanged, drooling mouth.

"Gimme an 'R' . . . "

I grabbed my toast from its plate and clutched it to my chest.

"Gimme an 'A' . . . "

"This?" I said, holding up the nearly-burned bread, its toasty fragrance overpowered by the fart stink.

"*NO*, TINY, DEFENSELESS, HUMAN NEW KID – I WANT YOUR TRAY!"

"There's a whole stack of them—"

"Gimme a 'Z' . . . "

"Just give him the tray, you idiot," Jessica hissed.

"Ohhhhh, you're *Graz*," I said. "Well, in that case, I'm not really hungry for that tray – be my guest."

The six-hundred-pound beast with T-Rex teeth snatched my breakfast tray away and took a massive bite. As the plastic splinters showered down into my hair, I realized conspiracy theorists might actually be right about something.

I knew what Groom Lake was rumored to be – Google it and you get Area 51, the secret air base that was supposedly home to alien cover-ups. But up until now I'd dismissed it as a made-up myth like the Loch Ness monster, the tooth fairy, or Justin Bieber's talent.

But that morning I learned there was a big difference between conspiracy theory and conspiracy reality.

Aliens were real. And they lived among us. Or rather, we now lived among them.

CHAPTER FOUR

Close Encounters

From their stations on the wall, the fungi kids described my alien encounter like commentators on a prize fight.

"The Big Fuzz is gonna pulverize the cumin beans!" called one of the wall-mounted mushrooms.

"You mean Human Beings, genius," snapped its neighbor.

I tried to tune out their cackles and was left with Graz's raspy breathing. I could feel every bulging eye and antenna in the cafeteria flit from Jessica to me, Jessica to me, Jessica to me . . .

. . . to something else.

Something I couldn't see yet. Something that was apparently approaching from behind the tray-eating monster. Something all the creature-kids suddenly couldn't take their eyes off.

"Oh my *Me* . . . " the something sneered in a snooty

voice. "It appears that Meltzer is letting *anyone* into this place now."

From behind Graz, a glowing white, human-ish figure stepped into view and folded his arms. Clad in a shimmery, iridescent cloak, he stood cool-as-ice casual beside the furry monster's thigh. He looked like a living mannequin, and the first word that came to me was:

Expensive.

His cloak floated like it was underwater; strangely mesmerizing, but also menacing. His face, hair and skin all looked like pale china and his emerald-green eyes glowed with contempt.

Every school had one – this guy must be Groom Lake's resident rich kid.

I could imagine a gang of space-slaves ironing his cape every morning, and a hovering space-limo dropping him off at the front steps each day.

"Grazzat," he said. "I'd like a closer look at these mortals."

Before I could protest, Graz's claws closed around my ankles and the horizon turned upside down. For a couple of seconds I just hung there, gazing wistfully at my French toast which had fallen to the floor.

"Put him *down* or no lunch for you!" Nancy hollered from behind her counter. "Ms Teg! Ms Teg, where are you? There are shenanigans here! Shenanigans like you wouldn't believe!"

The shimmer-kid took a couple of steps towards me, looked me up and down, or from my point of view, down and up, and scowled.

"Do they have names?" he said. "These *indigenous* . . . life forms?"

"Put me down, you Goose smell-a-like," I said, thrashing around in Graz's grip, trying to wriggle free, but to absolutely no effect.

"Sherman, just stay still and ride it out," snapped Jessica in a bored voice – she'd been witness to several similar first-day rituals. It wasn't exactly an alien experience for me, except that this time . . . it was.

"*Sher*-man," the shimmer-kid said. "I'd hardly call you a man."

"Then what are *you*?"

"I am a deity, a god of the galaxy," he boasted. "Ruler of the Aristox quadrant and rightful occupier of the cool seniors' table. You look like a freshman nobody, who needs to be reminded of his place in the universal pecking order."

He turned to the fuzz-monster and said, "Grazzat,

since this *Sher*-man is new here, I think perhaps we should show this *Sher*-man where he belongs."

Graz hoisted me higher as he strode over to three aluminum barrels full of leftover "food" that were in the front corner of the cafeteria, perfectly positioned for everyone to witness my debut humiliation.

"If you're going to toss him in," Jess said, "at least drop him in the squishy stuff and not in the ... are those *rocks*?"

"You're not helping, Jess!" I said.

"*Eeee-oww*," she squealed as Graz reached down with his other hairy arm and scooped her up too.

"I'm going to *murder* you, Sherman Capote," she threatened. "Twice!"

And there we hung, the new Capote kids, the only two human pupils at Groom Lake High. We hovered helplessly over a garbage can of discarded alien foodstuffs and waited to plummet. Nobody came to our aid, not one single species. I guessed none of the other aliens dared to stand up to Graz and the shimmer-kid.

Not the fungal hyenas.

Not the bendy cylinder kids.

Not the slugs.

Not even the ninja flowers.

Nobody.

The technical term for this is "bystander non-intervention". I looked it up later. But right then, hanging upside down from a stinking, hairy claw, I simply knew it as "another first day of school".

CHAPTER FIVE

Better Late Than NED

Groom Lake may have been a new school, but getting bullied was an old ritual. Graz shook us like upside-down maracas and I had braced myself for trash impact when suddenly, the shaking stopped.

"You've filled your bully quota, fuzzface," called a female voice from behind me.

"Move it, pinky," Graz growled, "or I'll dunk you too."

I twisted around to try to catch a glimpse of who he was growling at, and spotted a five-foot pink lizard in glossy black overalls. She was glaring, hands on hips. And she was actually kind of cute; you know, in a rose-hued-iguana kind of way.

"The name's Sonya," she said to the monster. "Or is that too many syllables for you?"

"Who you callin' silly?" he spat.

Sonya suddenly slammed all three lids closed, leaped

on top of the center one and folded her arms like she meant business. Three green tongues flicked from between her lips.

"Not a good move, Aristox," said the shimmer-kid.

"Don't mind NED," Sonya said to me. "He just *acts* like he owns the place."

"He owns your planet's *Ballet-thingy*," Graz grunted.

"It's *Balleropera*," Sonya said. "I *know* that's too many syllables for you."

She turned back to me. "It's not like we *choose* to spend our lives learning dances for the creepiest deities around." She rolled her eyes towards the shimmer-kid – NED.

"Bite those tongues, reptile," NED hissed. "One day, your little pink family will be performing for *me*. I'd hate to be . . . displeased."

Sonya clenched her fists, and her black eyes bulged. I could tell she was holding back the urge to continue her rant.

"Good little lizard," NED said.

Graz flipped the barrel lid to Sonya's left, grabbed me in the crook of his elbow and raised me back into the air above the slimy alien leftovers. Jessica was still trapped in Graz's left hand, like a goth version of Fay Wray in King Kong's clutches. He curled me up into his stinking, hairy armpit and grabbed Sonya, my would-be savior, by her collar. Now all three of us were dangling in the air above the refuse.

"Thanks, Sonya," I said, wanting to introduce myself before being covered in trash. "I'm Sherman."

"No probs, newbie," she said. "There's showers in the locker rooms off the gym. Round the corner on the left."

"Oh, good to know," I said. And it was. At my other schools, I'd been egged, toilet-papered and, in Korea, kimchied.

"Drop them, Grazzat," NED ordered.

I closed my eyes, covered my head.

And fell.

Until a giant python caught me.

CHAPTER SIX

Saved by a Tentacle

Hanging in the air, eyes closed, I listened for some clue that, if I opened them, I wasn't going to regret it.

"*AAAAAAACHOO.*"

It was Sneeze-zilla. Sneeze-point-eight on the Richter scale. The Sneeze had saved me. I decided that maybe it was safe to look.

"Octo?"

All I could see were tentacles. Everywhere.

Blue tentacles with yellow tiger-stripes snaked in the air all around me. Some wrapped around the three of us, suspending us above the garbage cans, while others curled around Graz's arms and legs and middle, hoisting him – raging and roaring – high off the ground.

"Leave 'em alone," Octo said. I followed the twisting tentacles to the source of the deep voice: a bulbous squid's head, massive and blue. Octo had two green eyes with huge, rectangular pupils, and three giant beaks.

"GET YOUR OCTOPUS TENTACLES OFF ME," Graz snarled.

"It's *ventitent*," Octo said, "not *octopus*. Twenty tentacles. Or can you not count that high?"

"He's not great with syllables or counting," Sonya said.

I looked down – Octo definitely had more than eight tentacles, but they were writhing around so much it was hard to keep count. Beyond the weaving striped snakes, I noticed NED backing away into the crowd. He was still looking full of himself, but clearly wanted to avoid an outright confrontation with the cephalopod.

"VENTI-*WHAT*?" Graz growled.

"Just chill out, Graz," Octo said, "and play *nice*."

"FORGET IT, SUCKERFINGERS."

A tentacle swung up and slapped Graz like a plaything. Octo then lowered all of us to the floor. Graz didn't try to retaliate. The furry bully was outgunned by Octo's twenty python arms.

I gave Sonya the most relaxed smile I could, considering I'd just been fearing for my life.

"Thanks for standing up for me," I said.

"I wasn't standing up for you," she said sharply. "I was standing up for the Aristox who've been controlled by NEDs for thousands of years, for emancipation, for freedom, for—"

Brrrrrrring!

The bell rang – a completely normal school bell . . . *weird* – and everybody but Octo, Jessica and I shuffled out of the cafeteria.

"Sherman the new kid, right?" boomed Octo. "Way to start a new school in style."

"Nice to meet you, in person I mean," I said, knowing that *person* wasn't exactly the right word.

He stuck out a tentacle. It had one of those rubber sports bracelets on it. In fact, all twenty tentacles had one, each a different color. I shook the blue-and-yellow tentacle, hoping that was the idea. It was surprisingly warm, and not as slimy as I'd suspected.

"Uh, yeah, thanks," said Jessica, straightening her black skirt over her jeans and refastening her faux-diamond skull hairclip.

"WHOA," said Octo. "You said you had a *cute* sister, but—"

"Gross!" I protested. "I said I had an *acute* sister allergy." But Octo wasn't listening any more. He was fixated on Jess.

"What's your first class, baby-cakes?"

"Drama," she said. "And call me baby-cakes again and I'll find a sushi chef to deal with you."

"Touché," he said, sticking out a tentacle to shake

Jess's hand. "That's French for touch. And touch you may."

Jessica sighed, holding out her right pinky finger and tapping the tentacle.

I pulled my timetable from my pocket and quickly realized the morning was about to go from bad to worse. I had Drama as well. It was my absolute least favorite subject.

"You know what time it is, Sherman?" Jessica said as the three of us paced the corridors – Octo also had Drama. "It's eight twenty-five. That's all. We still have a whole *day* of this insanity to live through."

"Don't mind Jessica, she's the queen of the drama queens," I said.

"Oh, I don't mind her," Octo said. "I don't mind Her Majesty at all."

The twenty-tentacled alien, who'd just saved my bacon, was actually digging my sister. It was the strangest discovery so far that someone, from any galaxy, had a crush on Jessica.

But it was about to get a whole lot stranger.

CHAPTER SEVEN

Drama King

Jessica and I half-jogged to keep pace with Octo as the ventitent cruised though the crowd, one tentacle curled up to hold his backpack in place as he navigated the busy hallway.

The sights were extraordinary – chattering creatures walking, snaking, slithering, hovering and galloping to their classes – but the sounds were totally normal, the soundtrack of any other school: keys jangling, locker doors slamming, sneakers squeaking on waxed floor tiles. It was like my eyes and ears weren't part of the same head.

"You realize you're the only human kids here, right?"

It was quite a thought.

I'd spent a year as the only American boy at an off-base school in South Korea (and I was used to being the only kid interested in rockets and propulsion no matter *what* school I was in), but being the only human male in the student body made me feel . . . well . . .

Alien.

As we walked, dodging jet-powered paper airplanes and the occasional pigskin, the insectoids, reptiles, robots, and creatures that defied conventional classification sized us up.

I was used to this walk – I call it "the catwalk". I usually hated it, but here it was almost a relief getting eyeballed because we were descended from apes, not because our clothes or hair didn't follow a local fashion trend.

I decided to treat this like any other first day of school. I'd just try to survive it.

"So, what's your story?" Octo asked. "Why are you guys at Groom Lake?"

"*Our* story?" gasped Jessica. "You're kidding, right? What's *your* story, tentacles?"

"I asked first, lollipop," Octo laughed.

"It's just one big geopolitical misunderstanding," I began, trying to change the subject to stop any flirting between the walking squid and my sister.

"It's all his fault!" she said, jabbing a finger in my ribs.

"It's a long, complicated story," I said. "And it's kind of funny when you—"

"It's a short, straightforward story," Jessica said. "With a tragic ending."

I explained that our dad had been stationed at the NATO base in Germany and that he'd suddenly been transferred to Groom Lake.

"More like grounded in Groom Lake," said Jess.

"Just your average, always-on-the-move, Air-Force-brats scenario," I said.

"But tell him *why* Dad got transferred," Jessica said. "Tell him why Dad got demoted. Tell him why we got kicked out of *Europe*."

I looked from Jessica to Octo and back – from Jessica's pursed lips and one-of-these-days-revenge-will-be-mine glare to Octo's glassy green eyes and oversized beaks – took a breath and spilled the beans.

"There was kind of an . . . incident," I said.

"Involving a missile!"

"Involving a *rocket*," I clarified. "That I built."

"Your science project exploded or something?" Octo asked, his eyes widening.

"If only," Jessica muttered.

"It was a little more advanced than that," I explained. "My rockets are *always* a little more advanced than that."

"So, okay," Octo said, "you're an egghead. Being an egghead doesn't get you kicked out of Europe."

"He's a mad scientist," Jessica snarled. "Being a mad

scientist who almost starts World War Three gets you kicked out of a two-thousand-mile radius of Russian airspace."

I had to set the record straight. "I'm not mad! Yeah, I like science. But I wouldn't call myself a scientist, yet. I'm more like a rocketry savant, the kind of—"

"Oh, give it a rest, Sherman!"

"A rocketry what?" Octo asked.

"Savant," I said. "Kind of like Mozart, but with boosters and guidance systems instead of violins and sheet music."

"I'm not familiar with Moat's Art," said Octo, "but I'm sure it's lovely."

"I have serious misgivings," Jessica scoffed, "about the quality of education we're about to receive here. You don't know Mozart? Beethoven? Bach?"

"Nope."

"How about Homer?"

Octo nodded enthusiastically. "Love-love-love *The Simpsons*. Hey, so how come you guys aren't more, you know, yellow?"

Jessica ignored him. "How about Shakespeare? Ever heard of him?"

"Oh, man," Octo said, "not *that* guy. We'll get enough of him in *here*."

The sign above the silver double doors said AUDITORIUM. Octo curled a tentacle around Jessica's shoulder.

"Ever tread the boards, baby-ca—?" he said, before cutting himself off. He'd obviously taken Jessica's sushi threat seriously.

"At our last school, in Germany," she said, "which I really liked – kind of loved, actually – I had the lead in *Beauty and the Beast*."

Octo raised a cephalopod eyebrow.

"Aren't you curious which one she was?" I asked. But Octo wasn't taking the bait.

"Good to know," he said to me, "open to inter-species dating."

I rolled my eyes as Octo turned back to Jess and said, "I bet you got a standing ovation."

"I'll never know," she said. "The premiere was last night. I was in the middle of my opening number when the alarm sounded. Instead of getting a standing ovation, I got sent here. Under armed guard. Because of *him*."

She shook off Octo's tentacle, and marched into the auditorium.

"What did you do, buckaroo?"

The silver doors of the auditorium opened again, just a little, and a giant insect poked its head out.

Even after a morning filled with surprises, that made me jump.

"I am Ms Teg and you young thespians are tardy," said the six-foot, winged praying mantis in a black trouser suit. I relaxed as soon as I realized this creature was planning to teach us, not eat us.

She led us into the cavernous auditorium, clicking her high-heeled hind claws and giving her wings a flutter.

"Let us *not* keep the Bard waiting one moment longer," she announced in a whispery chorus, like three people were saying the words.

After the cafeteria, I'd expected big things from the auditorium – more glass and chrome and cool lighting – but it was kind of a dump: threadbare maroon curtains, creaky varnished floorboards and rows of ancient, cracked, built-in chairs. Even though it was as clean and tidy as everywhere else, the whole room felt neglected and unloved.

The rest of the class, a variety of about twenty creatures, mooched around onstage, chatting and texting. I recognized a few of the species from the cafeteria – a potted pansy, a willowy bendy kid and a tiny snail creature. There was no Sonya to say hello to, but fortunately no Graz or NED either.

Jessica jumped onto the stage, rushed into the center

and smiled. It was the most content she'd looked all day. I was the complete opposite. The whole drama thing gave me the heebie-jeebies. There was something unsettling and unnatural about standing on a stage in front of people – or aliens – pretending to be someone you're not.

So I approached the stage as slowly as I could.

"Earth to Sherman," said Octo, who was still waiting for an answer to his question. "*What* did you do?"

"According to NATO, World War Two nearly got a sequel," I said. "The Russians tracked the rocket from Geilenkirchen into their airspace. All *they* knew was it was a missile, fired from a NATO base, heading right for them. I mean, if they'd decided to fire back . . . Well, we wouldn't be standing here right now."

"But why'd you get shipped to *Groom Lake*?" Octo said.

"I guess this is where the Air Force hides the secrets it doesn't want the world to know about," I said, gesturing to the aliens onstage, then pointing to him and me with a shrug.

"So no more fireworks?" he asked, miming an explosion with at least fifteen of his tentacles.

"According to Article Five of the Geilenkirchen settlement," I recited, "NATO will hand me over to the

Russians to rot in a gulag if I ever touch another rocket."

Octo slapped me on the back. "Mighty impressive, buckaroo!"

"Boys, boys, boys, less chitter-chatter," Ms Teg said. "Join your fellow thespians on the stage and *listen*."

Octo and I climbed the wooden steps to the stage and watched Ms Teg straighten her jacket, take a breath and begin. Her voice – rather, her *voices* – echoed around the theatre, filling the neglected space with iambic pentameter.

> *But, soft! what light through yonder window breaks?*
> *It is the east, and Juliet is the sun.*

It sounded pretty amazing – even the little-gray-men guys stopped babbling and listened – and Jessica just *drank* it up, her eyes alight.

> *Arise, fair sun, and kill the envious moon,*
> *Who is already sick and pale with grief . . .*

What was weird, though, was the glow that appeared in the air above Ms Teg. A spherical, glimmering little sky-blue cloud. Out of nowhere.

> *That thou her maid art far more fair than she:*
> *Be not her maid, since she is envious . . .*

The cloud-ball thing was growing arms and legs, and then a head. Like a glowing snow angel hovering in the air.

Her vestal livery is but sick and green
And none but fools do wear it; cast it off.

"What's *that*?" I whispered to Octo.

"*Who's* that," Octo said with a wink. "You're gonna love what comes next."

At the time, I had no idea how right he was.

CHAPTER EIGHT

Volunteerism

The blue cloud became a girl. She floated there, iridescent, semi-transparent, like she was made of turquoise crystal. I had to squint my eyes a little to look, and when I did, I couldn't miss how breathtakingly, ridiculously beautiful she was.

Ms Teg tutted and glared up at her.

"If you're going to float in and out of classes," she said, "it would behoove you to remember that my class starts at eight forty-five sharp."

The girl nodded, then gave Ms Teg a *dazzlingly* cute smile.

"Good," Ms Teg said. "Now to Shakespeare! Nothing like the Bard in the entire universe. . ."

She went on and on – Stratford-upon-Avon, The Globe, *Romeo and Juliet,* the school play, casting, blah, blah, blah. I stopped listening because I was mesmerized by the gorgeous goddess floating on the stage, basking in her own blue aura.

"Er . . . who is—" I asked Octo.

"Don't waste your time, two-legs," Octo whispered. "She is way out of your league."

"I kind of guessed that," I said, "but who—"

"Out of your galaxy," Octo said.

"I get it," I said, "thanks for the encouragement. But seriously, what's her name?"

"I mean *literally* out of your galaxy," he said. "You know what 'omnipotent' means?"

I didn't, but I pretended I did and gave him Jessica's patented what-do-you-take-me-for look. But it turns out ventitents are pretty good at spotting a bluff, and he explained that omnipotent meant "all-powerful".

"She's a deity in training – an *Icon*," Octo said. "Icons are so *all-powerful* they don't *have* names."

"You mean she's a goddess – literally?" I whispered. "What's she doing in *school*?"

"She's not just in school," he said. "She's not just *here*. She's in a thousand places at once, and never anywhere for very long."

I continued to stare. There wasn't anything about her that seemed all-powerful or whatever; she was just, quite simply, gorgeous. Like a floating fashion model. A transparent, teenage Tinkerbell – minus the wings. She was perfection personified . . . in alien form.

"A thousand places at once?" I said.

"Exactly," Octo said. "Which means right now there's a thousand other doofuses just like you checking her out and getting all mushy-mushy. So cool your rocket booster, Mr Savant."

"Understood," I said, pretending to understand.

"I hope so, buckaroo," Octo said, "because she ignores them completely. All of them. In fact, if you only learn one thing today, make it this: Icons ignore doofuses."

"Then how come," I said, "she's smiling at this particular doofus?"

She was. Definitely. She might have been in a thousand different worlds but she was smiling at me – one Sherman Capote, new resident of Groom Lake, Nevada, Earth.

"Holy sea-cow," Octo gasped. "She *is*."

It felt like being on a rollercoaster. In summer. The day school finishes.

"You gotta bust out your opening moves," Octo said. "You do have moves, dontcha?"

"Not really," I confessed, hoping that maybe a simple, nonchalant wave might be the safest gesture, unless of course it meant something different to an alien deity. "I'm going to wave. How does that sound?"

"If that's all you've got," Octo whispered, "go for it, two-legs."

I smiled back at her, looked into her crystal eyes and raised my hand. Cool as ice. I was so *non*chalant I was anti-chalant. I was protesting the chalant regime. I was an enemy of the chalant state.

"Why, thank you for volunteering, Mr Capote," Ms Teg cooed. "You'll make a wonderful Romeo."

Volunteering?

Romeo?

It took a few seconds for her words to sink in, for my brain to recalibrate from gushy-for-goddess to drama-class-drudgery.

"I'm sorry, Ms Teg – what?" I asked. "A wonderful what?"

"Yes, a truly captivating Romeo," Ms Teg said. "That lovelorn expression is just perfect! A disciple of the Method, are we?"

Uh oh.

Please no.

"But he *hates* drama," Jessica protested, striding over and grabbing me by my vintage Carl Sagan T-shirt. "Tell her! You *hate* drama. Cluck-cluck-cluck."

My last major performance was as Chicken #3 in an off-off-off-Broadway production of *Old MacDonald's Farm*. But when my big moment came for a cluck-cluck-here and a cluck-cluck-there, I up-chucked here, there, and everywhere. I covered the farm in puke, including Jess who was busy stealing the show as Mrs MacDonald, the brains behind the MacDonald farming empire. It was the beginning and end of my child-acting career and Jessica has never forgiven nor forgotten.

She continued protesting, and then punched me on the arm.

"Ouch!" I cried. "That's my Nurse Anderson arm. What's your problem?"

"Let's keep the stage fighting to act three, scene one," Ms Teg snapped. "Now to cast our Juliet. Any volunteers?"

"My *problem* is," Jessica said, sneering at me behind her eyeliner overdose, "there's no way I'm volunteering to play star-crossed lover to my own *brother*. Why'd you have to stick your stupid hand up? Drama is, like, *the* class I love at school and you know it! And you've totally sabotaged it for me. On the first *day*!"

Meanwhile, Octo slapped me on the back so hard I nearly toppled offstage. He pointed a tentacle at the teacher.

"Thank you so much for volunteering, my dear," Ms Teg was saying, gazing up at the Icon girl. "You'll make a simply *exquisite* Juliet. But forgive me – remind me of your name?"

"*What's in a name?*" Icon-girl said. "*That which we call a rose by any other name would smell as sweet.*"

"Marvellous!" Ms Teg shrieked. "Divine! But, forgive me, I still need a name . . . for the playbill, you see."

"Juliet," Icon-girl said. "You can call me Juliet."

"Wonderful," said Ms Teg. "I trained with Strasberg and it's a privilege to work with a fellow disciple. And I'm sure you and Sherman will be brilliant together – I can already sense the chemistry."

I felt my face glow bright red and Octo nudged me.

"Way to make an entrance, buckaroo," he whispered. "Quite a debut."

And it was.

CHAPTER NINE

Homework Bound

The air-raid siren started just as Octo, Jessica and I braved the hallway crowd outside the auditorium. The last time I'd heard that piercing sound, military police rushed me from all sides, pushed me from my launch pad and threw me to the ground.

"I didn't do anything," I shouted.

Octo put a reassuring tentacle around my shoulder and laughed.

"Don't sweat it!" he shouted over the wail, "it's just an alien invasion!"

"A *what*?" I yelled back, aiming for the little elliptical holes in the side of Octo's head.

"Well, a drill for alien invasion, anyway," he added. "They test it every Monday at ten."

And then the siren stopped.

I watched the mass of extraterrestrials bustling down the hallway, making their way from first period to second as if the siren were as normal as a PA announcement about the cancellation of Chess Club.

"Surely it's too late for sirens," I quipped, looking around at the swarm of alien life moving between classes. "It feels to me like you've already invaded."

"But you can't assume every space-schlepper who shows up in a star-cruiser wants to join our friendly desert melting pot," Octo explained, earnestly. "It's the Bureau's job to be ready in case anyone or anything turns up with more butt-kicking intentions than enrolling their kids in Groom Lake High."

"The Bureau?"

"Yeah, you know, the Bureau for Alien Affairs. All of our parents work for the Bureau, including your dad now, right?"

"He used to be a four-star general," Jessica said. "Now he's working for aliens?"

"*With* aliens," said Octo. "All of the adults work for the Bureau, and by Nevada State law, all of us offspring have to attend school until we turn eighteen . . . in Earth years, that is."

I couldn't help laughing. "So extraterrestrials can cross all the time and space of the universe but can't get out of homework?"

"Nope," said Octo. "And we'd better not be late for next class or Mr Orson will assign us plenty."

"Oh, great," Jessica said. "It's my class too. Just promise me you won't ruin my life again."

Given what happened next, I was glad I didn't make that promise.

★ ★ ★

My timetable told me that the curriculum at Groom Lake was a blend of basic Earth stand-by subjects (Math, English, Science, Drama, Home Economics, PE) plus stuff *these* guys might need to get into colleges throughout the universe; subjects like Intergalactic Physics and Astro-Mechanics, Galactic Languages, and Planetology – our next class.

The teacher, Mr Orson, was a rock.

Literally.

He looked like a sandstone take on a snowman, and when he moved he made a sound like bricks being rubbed together. He wore a sharp suit, bow tie, and green handkerchief in his breast pocket – like he'd rather be a university professor than a school teacher.

From the look of the lab, it was pretty clear that Planetology was the kind of subject Groom Lake High *did* like to spend its money on. A new-carpet smell, the same super-flash computers as Mr Meltzer's, tables that were little baby versions of the cafeteria's hexagons . . . *this* was school in style.

Jessica took an empty seat at the back, near the row of windows overlooking the manicured front lawn and row of beige Groom Lake bungalows. I followed Octo to a table on the far right. We were soon joined by Sonya and a silver robot who seemed to be sulking as he slid into his seat.

"You survived your first class," said Sonya. I couldn't tell if it was a question or a statement.

"Survived and thrived," laughed Octo.

"Who's the newbie?" the silver robot asked in a disinterested, digital voice.

"His name's Sherman," said Octo, "and I'm being nice to him to get to his hot sister." He pointed to Jessica at the back, and that's when I spotted NED seated two tables over from her. Oh, *great*.

"There is so much wrong with what he just said, I don't even know where to begin," I said. "But nice to meet you."

"Whatever," the robot muttered.

"Don't mind Houston, he's been in a perma-grump since he came to Groom Lake," said Sonya. "At least you're not the new kid any more, Metal Man."

Houston was sleek like a brushed-steel Japanese car, but teenage-boy-shaped, with little camera lenses for eyes. His voice, although fully digital, somehow seemed very sad.

"You're different from the other robots," I said, thinking back to the yellow-and-black techno-playing bots from the cafeteria.

"And you're different from the model of perfection that my television tells me to expect from the human race," he said.

"Do we have a problem, Houston?" snapped Mr Orson.

"No, sir, just introducing myself to the newest minnow in the shark tank."

"No more interruptions then," said our sandstone instructor, returning to the surprisingly old-school chalkboard and diagraming a volcanic system using his finger as the chalk. The low-screech sound gave me shivers.

"I'm not originally of robotic form," Houston said cryptically. I wanted to ask what he meant but Octo cut in.

"You guys'll never believe what happened in Drama this morning. Two-legs here got cast as Romeo and guess who he's star-crossed with? The Icon!"

"Did she actually talk to you?" asked Houston, suddenly more animated.

"She'll never stick around for opening night," said Sonya. "Better get used to performing monologues."

Mr Orson scratched his rocky fingers across the board, assaulting our ears and calling for silence.

"If you have time to chinwag," he said, "you have time to spare. Congratulations – your table has won the privilege!"

His fingers tapped keys on his computer until, in the air above us, a breathtaking 3D hologram of the Earth pixelated into existence – continents, oceans, clouds – with a dazzling red sphere glowing at its center.

"Next session," he announced, "these four talkative folk will give a presentation to the class about the Earth's magma core. A golden opportunity to investigate the geology of this remarkable planet."

"Nice one, thanks, Octo," Sonya said.

"Great," Houston declared flatly.

"It's his fault," Octo said, waving a tentacle at me.

But I just grinned. "Did I mention that I'm playing Romeo opposite an *Icon*?"

"Kiss my excretion valve, two-legs," he said, smiling with all three beaks.

"Mr Orson?" piped up a familiarly sickening voice from the back. NED. "Did you say *magma*?"

The teacher nodded – it sounded like stones grinding.

"Then I volunteer to join their homework assignment."

"That's very granite-like of you, NED," said the rock. "I wish everyone in this class was so enthusiastic about planetary geology."

"What's going on?" I whispered to Sonya.

"Beats me. The only thing NED ever volunteers for is insulting people."

* * *

At the end of class, NED sidled up to our table with a creepy grin.

"Why don't we make this homework assignment less theoretical and more practical?"

"You mean like throw you into a volcano?" snapped Sonya.

"Sure," said NED, with a snide giggle. "I thought a field trip might be a lark. We could visit a real volcano and report back with photos and first-hand knowledge. You know, really dazzle Mr Orson with our initiative."

"Who says we weren't going to do that anyway? But I'm not driving you nowhere, NED," said Octo.

"Grammatically," he replied, "you just offered to drive me anywhere."

"Double negative," cursed Octo under his breath. "Why does human-talk have to be so complex?"

"But, anyway, who said anything about driving?" NED continued. "How 'bout it, lizard, I hear you've got a spaceship."

My jaw dropped. "Really?" I asked Sonya.

"Why don't you take us on a little trip," suggested NED, "down to Costa Rica? Robo-boy here could take holographs and you could show off your piloting skills in front of the human."

"I'm in if we can get drive-thru," Octo said. "Or fly-thru."

"Why should I, NED?" asked Sonya.

"Well, you don't have to, but maybe I'll call my father and ask him to summon your family to perform a little dance number for the elders. And you know what the punishment is for even a single misstep."

"Yes," she sighed, lowering her eyes.

"Tell *Sher*-man," he said with malice.

"Death," she whispered, almost inaudibly.

NED pulled out a super-slick neon phone and started tapping digits.

"Okay, I'll do it," she said. "Meet us in the scrapyard at eight. Don't be late."

"Tootles," said NED, strolling off to his next class.

"Um, Sonya," I said. "Can I ask you a question?"

"Look, the dance thing is an ancient tradition," she said defensively. "I don't expect you to understand."

And with that she huffed off, shaking her head.

"I can't go," I said to Octo and Houston. "I'm not allowed to touch rockets."

Octo chuckled. "You'll be fine then. You'll just wish her ship was a rocket. Catchya later, buckaroo."

CHAPTER TEN

That Lunchtime Feeling

After third period – Math for me, English for Jess – the lunchtime cafeteria was packed with hungry extraterrestrials. The fungi kids struggled to heckle above the roar of aliens gossiping in unintelligible languages, but it didn't stop them from narrating my arrival.

"The cumin bean survived the morning!"

"Eeewww – what's he gonna eat? Is that really food?"

"What do you think of our circus so far?" asked Nancy as she scooped some perfectly cooked, golden french fries onto a plate. She poured steaming gravy on top and slid my lunch onto my tray.

"It's pretty mind-boggling how quickly you start to get used to things," I said, looking around nervously, happy not to spot Graz.

"Tell me about it," Nancy laughed. "Spoiled brats are spoiled brats the galaxy over. Fangs or no fangs. Antennae or no antennae. Keep the line moving, kiddo."

I laughed too, because it was true. And then I stopped laughing because it was time to find a seat.

This was always my least favorite part of the school day; the time when the universe reminded me I had no one to sit with. In Germany and Korea I went home for lunch, where Mom would have left me a sandwich or some rocket-shaped pasta to heat up, but here I was under strict lock-in until the three-thirty bell. I flicked my eyes around the cafeteria, hoping to find my Planetology crew, or at the very least Jessica.

"Would you look at that," Nancy whistled. "Looks like you've got yerself a blue admirer." She pointed towards a corner table at the far side of the cafeteria, one of four on a raised platform overlooking the plebs below.

Juliet was smiling at me and waving me over to the empty chair next to her.

Rollercoaster.

Sunshine.

Birds singing.

I gave a small wave back (careful not to volunteer for anything else) and, with my heart thumping out of my chest, made my most casual approach.

She was mesmerizing. I couldn't take my eyes off her. She looked stunning, surrounded by her translucent blue glow as she surveyed the chaos of the cafeteria. It was only when I stepped up onto the platform, two feet above the rest of the lunch room, that I noticed Graz and NED were sitting at her table.

"This table's invitation only, *Sher*-man," announced NED.

"He's new," said Juliet. "He can sit with us."

Graz stood up, towering over me menacingly while drooling at the sight of my tray. The last thing I needed was a repeat of the garbage can incident – this time in front of Juliet.

"This is the cool seniors' table," NED oozed as he put his arm around Juliet in a possessive, "don't look at my super-smokin', translucent blue girlfriend" kind of way. "And the *Sher*-man is neither cool nor a senior."

By this time the entire cafeteria was watching my attempt at social climbing, and I heard pitying laughter from all around the room. I backed down. I would have blamed it on the rapidly cooling fries, but the truth was I really didn't want to be hung upside down twice in one day.

As I retreated backward down the steps with my tray, I felt a tickle on the back of my neck. I turned round to find Octo's tentacle tapping me.

"C'mon, newbie," he said. "So long as you're not having the calamari, you dine with me."

I followed Octo to an empty table at the other side of the cafeteria, in a kind of lunch room hinterland. When I looked back, Juliet had vanished.

"Where'd she go?" I wondered aloud, sitting opposite the ventitent. He held his bowl up to one of his beaks and slurped something black and slimy through a thick straw.

"I told you," he said, gulping down the goo. "That's what she does. A thousand places at once. The Icons are like gods – they're expected to be watching over the universe all the time."

"So is NED the same?" I asked. "He says he's a deity – he certainly acts like he thinks he's a god but—"

"He's a minor deity who wants to be major," explained Octo. "You see, the Icons let the NEDs have some free rein because they go back a long way. They're like the aristocracy of the universe, and they all take care of each other."

"So maybe I shouldn't have backed down in front of Juliet?" I wondered.

"Listen," Octo began. "You're at Groom Lake High School now, not a fancy-pants school in Euroland. There's a hierarchy to this place. And *you* just tried to crash the cool seniors' table. That's like upsetting the balance of the entire universe. It's just not done."

Without looking up from his slime, Octo used a tentacle as a pointer and gave me the lowdown, one table at a time.

The raised platform housed four tables: the cool seniors ("jerks"), the cool juniors ("jerks-in-waiting"), the yearbook committee ("harmless but plugged in") and the cafeteria monitors (Ms Teg and another praying mantis lady who were picking at salads and marking papers).

Below them were the mere mortals who wished they were eating above the rest.

The AJABots: "Sturdy, dependable, hard-working, good taste in techno."

The Aristox: "The pink-lizard family with a cultlike devotion to their traditional dance ritual."

The Pansies: "Yep, the plant pot guys – do *not* mess with them or they will mess with you."

The football team: "Erudite, sophisticated, subtle – *hahahahahaha*."

The Fungi: "They never sit at their table, but it's still their turf – dude, avoid, or they'll never let you forget it."

The Martians: "Little-gray-men guys – not really Martians, but they're rocket guys, like you, good racers."

I wondered what "good racers" was all about, but kept listening.

"Then there's us, right here," Octo continued. "Welcome to Octo's Seafood Snack Bar. Behind you, your garden-variety Xenophine Reeds—"

Five of them billowed at their table, chattering to themselves. They rose, fell, and twisted as if they were dancing to their own unheard tunes.

"Behind them is the insect quarter," he said, pointing to two tables of giant-sized spiders, scorpions and caterpillars. "Then you've got your Slugs, and over there are your Fartulas."

"Fartulas?" I asked. "Those dumpy potato guys?"

"Do *not* sit at their table, okay?" Octo warned. "And don't ever sit downwind of them."

I tried to take it all in, keep it all straight in my spinning head. Octo laughed his gurgling, cephalopod laugh.

"You'll get it," he said.

"You think?"

"Just remember, there's a strict order to life here at Groom Lake High. Everyone in their place."

"It just doesn't seem fair."

"Fair? Ha! The whole system is rigged against you and punctuated by rituals designed to test your mettle: football games, the school play, Prom, Rocket Races—"

"Rocket Races, what's that?"

He laughed. "Like a moth to a flame, you! Rocket Races are the Groom Lake take on drag-car racing. You know, with rockets instead of cars. Speaking of, why weren't you at Rocket Camp today?"

Rocket Camp appeared to be the nickname for Intergalactic Physics and Astro-Mechanics, the class before lunch.

"I had Math instead," I confessed. "I'm not allowed to 'partake' in Astro-Mechanics, in case I get tempted to build anything . . . space-faring."

"You're a marked man, Capote," he chuckled. "A marked man."

CHAPTER ELEVEN

Pizza Night

That evening, Dad arrived from his first day at work in his general's formal dress, minus the decorations, holding a steaming box of *What Beats a Pizza?* pepperoni pie.

He popped his version of gourmet cooking onto the table, and summoned us to family mealtime.

"Did you learn anything new today at school, kids?" he asked, sounding like he was on autopilot.

I nearly choked on my slice. Was he kidding?

"I learned that just when I thought Sherman couldn't ruin my life any more," said Jessica, "he finds another way."

"I learned that ALIENS ARE REAL!" I shouted, hoping to get a reaction from Dad.

My father, former four-star general Frank Capote, had never really been the same since Mom died. He'd been drifting through the days in a kind of ambivalent fog, unfazed by anything. But if there was one thing I thought might snap him out of his funk, it'd be aliens on Earth.

"What did he do this time?" he asked Jessica.

"ALIENS!!!" I repeated.

"He totally sabotaged the play for me. I'm Lady Capulet because I can't be Juliet."

"Sherman to Dad! *Aliens!* On *Earth!*"

"Why not?" he asked.

"Living among us!"

"Because Sherm-eo here got the male lead."

"Technically, Sherman, in Groom Lake, it's we who live among *them*," my dad corrected. "And I thought you hated drama?"

"Arrgghhh!" said Jess. "This is about me, not him!"

"Dad," I said, "aren't you surprised, excited . . . I don't know, some kind of emotion?"

He loosened his tie and let out a breathy sigh.

"Sherman, when you get older, you'll come to appreciate that life is basically a series of disappointments. Yesterday I was a four-star general reporting to the Joint Chiefs. Today, I'm in charge of ordering stationery and reporting to a two-headed, walking iguana from outer space. Yesterday Jessica was starring as the lead in the school play, and today she's got a supporting role as an overprotective matron. Yesterday, Sherman, you were just a maladjusted fourteen-year-old, but today you're a wanted man for inciting global thermo-nuclear war."

I took a big bite of pizza. I needed pepperoni to get through Dad's sad-ologue.

"And yesterday I thought that human beings were the only intelligent species in the universe, not counting whales and dolphins, because they are smarter than most people give them credit for; but today, I know that humanity is just one little cluster on one little ant hill in one small corner of the universe. It's about lowering your expectations, and then lowering them some more. So, was I surprised to turn up for duty this morning and discover that the toilets were designed for those with alien anatomy? Yes. But mostly, I was disappointed. And not just because I had no place to pee."

Jessica and I stared at each other, both wondering who would be the first to break the awkward silence. I mouthed, *Is he okay?*

She shook her head, mouthing, *I don't think so*, and twirling her index finger in the universal hand gesture for crazy.

As much as we loathed one another, we also knew that we had only one parent left, and both of us were worried we might be losing him in his own Frank Capote way.

"Now, don't you kids have homework?"

Homework.

The magma mission.

"Actually," I said, "I have a group assignment for Planetology. But I, um, have to meet up with the others to do it."

Dad shot me a suspicious look.

"He does," Jessica said. "He got in trouble today for talking in class and has to give a presentation as punishment."

"You see: disappointment," said Dad. "Off you go, Sherman. Home by nine, no leaving base and, though it should go without saying, I'll say it anyway: no rockets of any kind."

I took a slice of pizza for the road and dashed out of the house, knowing I was about to break at least two of those rules.

CHAPTER TWELVE

Holy Flying Easter Egg

I followed the map Sonya had given me towards Area 51's scrapyard. As I walked through the quiet, residential part of the base, past identikit houses, I realized I'd never lived anywhere this hot before.

The warm, dry air reminded me of vacations when Mom was still alive. I remembered one trip, about four years ago, probably the last time I had been back to the States, when we all flew to Disney World. Jessica had gone gaga over the Magic Kingdom, but for me, the real highlight wasn't in Orlando, it was on the Atlantic coast: the Kennedy Space Center at Cape Canaveral. I marvelled at the rockets on display and Mom told me all about watching the Apollo missions when she was growing up. Jess couldn't drag us out of there for all the Dumbos at Disney.

My memorial rocket launch may have ended with Dad and Jess hating me, but I was still glad I'd launched Mom's ashes into space. Dad may have been disappointed in life, but it would have disappointed Mom if I hadn't tried to give her wings in death.

I picked up my pace to a light jog, passing the low bungalows that glowed from their living rooms' televisions. I spotted a family of giant worms curled up on the sofa watching a cop show and wondered what they must think of humanity's obsession with dramatizing murder in primetime. Across the street, a pair of six-armed apes desperately tried to soothe their crying baby. In another house, a family of AJABots haggled over Monopoly. Seeing all of these alien families made me wish that my family could be a bit more, well, normal.

But, like Dad said, maybe I needed to lower my expectations.

I followed the map across Groom Lake High's football field and kept to the edges, in the shadows. Then I climbed over a high fence in the end zone into the scrubby, parched stretch of desert between my new school and the outermost offices of the Bureau's military base.

The blinds were drawn on the two-floor beige office buildings and I snuck past without drawing attention to myself. The road dead-ended at a massive scrapyard of machinery, dilapidated hangars and rocket parts.

"*Psssst,*" someone whispered.

Sonya emerged from behind the office building, her pink face half-hidden in a hoodie but her reflective black eyes glinting in the moonlight.

"Come on," she whispered, and we ran into the yard. We weaved through piles of scrap that to anyone else would look like old jet parts and cargo containers – but to me, a self-trained rocket builder, these were ingredients for a gourmet space meal.

Gorgeous guidance systems.

Stranded starships.

Rusting rockets.

And *stacks* of silvery, metallic components that I couldn't quite identify – but they had my rocket-sense tingling like crazy.

"Sherman," Sonya asked, "are you licking your lips?"

"This is crazy!" I exclaimed. "Why would they leave all this great stuff out in the open?"

"Reverse psychology," Sonya speculated. "People assume anything out here can't be that important. It's genius. And it's a *great* place to hide the Eggcraft."

I'd assumed that her triple tongue gave her an occasional speech impediment and that she'd actually said "spacecraft". But no, once we rounded a corner, I saw it. And it was most definitely an egg.

An egg the size of a garbage truck.

An egg with two triangular cockpit windows, gold landing gear, exhaust pipes along the side like a dragster, and warm red light shining from an open hatch in the back, down onto the wire-mesh steps of the gangplank.

Houston, with eyes glowing orange and servos whirring softly, was running his silver fingers very slowly over the shell.

"Houston, why are you caressing my egg?" asked Sonya.

"I'm checking the hull for cracks," he said. "Better safe than . . . incinerated."

"Don't be such a downer," Sonya said. "She's solid."

I was trying to fathom the size of the chicken capable of laying this space-faring egg. "Can we go back to the *egg* part?" I asked.

"Come aboard," Sonya beckoned. "I'll show you how to fly her."

"No," Houston said. "Wait . . . " He straightened up, rotated his head and moved more robotically than I'd ever seen him move. "Vehicle approaching. Take cover."

Houston backed himself into the nearby space junk, switched off his eyes and disappeared. He was completely camouflaged amid the metallic cylinders and disused fuselages.

Sonya and I listened. All I could hear were the cicadas, and the breeze whistling through all that lovely space steel.

"Um, Houston," I said, "I don't hear—"

"*Shhh*," Sonya said, flicking her tongues. "I hear it too. Get *down*." She closed the hatch of the Eggcraft with a keyring remote, and dragged me over to join Houston.

From the darkness, we watched and we waited.

Finally, I heard the car. The chugging engine – louder and louder – of a four-by-four or maybe a truck. Its headlights reflected off the various rocket bodies until a bright red Toyota pick-up with no roof came into view, skidding to a halt. A familiar blue-and-yellow tentacle snaked out from the driver's side. And then another, and another . . .

"Bet you thought a ventitent couldn't drive one of these things, eh, bipeds?" Octo yelled.

He slammed the pick-up's door shut, all three of his beaks beaming with pride. "Um, bipeds?"

Sonya rolled her eyes and came out of hiding. "We're doing this in *secret*, remember?"

"What?" Octo shrugged. "You don't like my wheels?"

"You're telling me the guy with twenty legs couldn't just *walk*?" Sonya asked.

Houston had resumed his inspection of the egg, ignoring Octo.

"It's a style statement, and the ladies love it," he claimed. "Hiya, Houston, what's up?"

"*We* will be," he said, "at forty thousand feet, traveling over a thousand miles per hour, and I thought someone might appreciate a pre-flight hull integrity check before we take off."

"I keep telling you, the Eggcraft's solid," Sonya asserted.

"I can't believe you've got your own car," I said.

"Technically, it's my dad's," Octo explained. "Hank won it in a poker game but he can't stay out of the water long enough to drive it. So, it's now the Octo-mobile."

"You dad sounds awesome," I said.

"Hank's all right, but he'd *drown* me if he found out."

"Can we forget the ventitent's car, please?" Sonya said. "We have a volcano to study. Houston, are you satisfied?"

"Eggcraft hull," Houston said with a nod, "is ninety-eight-point-two-one-two-per cent sound."

"I smell pizza," Octo said, sniffing me. "I don't suppose you brought—"

"Rounding up, that's good enough for me," declared Sonya. She reopened the hatch with the chirp-chirp of her keyring clicker and leaped up the gangplank in what I swear was a ballet jump. "C'mon, if we take off now we can get out of here before NED finds us."

"Too late, Pinkberry," said a snobby voice from the darkness.

The deity-wannabe stepped out of the shadows, shimmering as he examined the giant egg. "But nobody said we'd be riding in . . . Oh, is that your birth-egg?" He screwed up his nose as if someone had farted.

"What?" Sonya hissed. "Not as shiny as the spaceship that daddy promised to buy you?"

"I can't think of *anything* more repulsive," NED said, "than a spaceship that came out of someone's—"

"But you're not invited," Sonya said.

"I want to be amused," he announced. "So make room. I'm coming with you."

"If you want to be amused, NED," said Sonya, "get a mirror. We're outta here."

"Then you'll all be expelled in the morning," he threatened. "Unauthorized departure from a classified facility is a serious offence."

"Are you kidding?" Sonya said. "The Eggcraft has a cloaking device. Makes her totally undetectable. Nobody's gonna find out a *thing*."

NED pulled his neon phone from his pocket, held

it up and – *FLASH* – took our photo. "Maybe I'll just email this right now to Meltzer. Or should I wait for the video of you mortals taking off?"

Sonya fumed. Octo froze.

"If I get expelled, dude," he explained, "I'll have to go back to the home planet, and that would not be good for my allergies."

"All right, NED, get aboard," said Sonya. "But don't expect me to amuse you."

NED sauntered up the gangplank, whistling "Leaving on a Jet Plane". I followed him into the ship and took my first look inside a bona fide spacecraft.

I tried to block out the fact that my least favorite alien was along for the ride, and that the egg came from a giant reptile's bottom.

I didn't want to lower my expectations.

CHAPTER THIRTEEN

Houston, We Have Lift-Off

The inside of the Eggcraft looked more like a trendy nightclub from Jessica's favorite TV show, *Drummer Girl*, than a spaceship.

The floor was flat and shiny, but the walls curved up into the ceiling, with portraits of what must be famous Aristox singers and movie stars. A row of red velvet benches was built into each side, with six small tables lining the central walkway to the cockpit, each with a vase holding a single flower. The whole chamber had a freshly-cut-grass smell, which kinda made sense, since it was one hundred per cent organic.

It was pretty amazing to think that in a few moments, I'd be who-knew-how-many thousands of feet up . . . in an *egg*.

"She's like my home away from home," Sonya said, disappearing into the cockpit through the front hatch.

Octo took up the entire bench on the left and Houston and NED took the right bench, distancing themselves from each other and leaving a space inbetween for me – one that I really didn't want to fill.

"Did you mean it?" I asked Sonya, peering into the cockpit. "About showing me how to fly this thing?"

"How to fly this *Eggcraft*," Sonya smiled, waving me in. "Welcome to the flight deck, Mr Capote."

The cockpit was minimalist chic with two blue-leather seats facing two chrome steering columns. The dashboard was cream-colored and smooth, no knobs or dials. Above the dash, two large triangular windshields gave us a great view of the rocket graveyard by moonlight.

Sonya had draped her hoodie over the back of her seat, revealing a T-shirt that read "Cold Blood, Warm Heart" above a funky, scratchy picture of a rock star – I guessed an Aristox one – playing a Fender Stratocaster, which was weird, I thought, it being an Earth guitar. It made me wonder if we used things on Earth that were alien and we just didn't know it. Microwave ovens? Maybe. Bluetooth? Probably. Those weird toilets you flush just by waving your hand at the sensor? *Definitely.*

The hatch hissed closed behind me, and I strapped myself in next to Sonya. Her skin, I realized, was the exact same color as Bubblicious gum, and you could only make out her little ladybug-sized scales if you really stared, so I tried not to. I was pretty sure that on her home planet, Sonya was seriously hot stuff.

"So is everybody playing nicely back there?" she asked.

"It's a bit tense for my liking," I said. "Octo and NED are doing that stare-down thing that boxers do before the bell rings."

"Do boxes have eyes on this planet?"

"Box*ers*," I clarified. "You know, two people punching each other? In a ring?"

Sonya looked at me with a frown of bewilderment.

"It's a sport," I explained.

"Hold on, human," she gasped. "Punching is a *sport* here?"

"Um, yeah, kind of tells you everything you need to know about humanity," I replied, realizing that I couldn't defend most of what passed for sports on this planet. "So, how do I fly this?"

She clapped her hands together and a rainbow-shaped, multi-colored virtual control panel *fizzed* instantly into life behind the steering columns. "Watch and learn."

"*Now* I feel like I'm in a spaceship."

Sonya ran her fingers through a blue hemisphere on the panel, and then leaned toward it.

"Buckle up, boys," she called.

I watched her hands glide through the virtual panel – tapping blue and pink holographic buttons.

"Activating start-up," she said.

A very subtle vibration kicked in under my feet and the whole egg seemed to hum.

"Okay," Sonya said. "Lesson one: Eggcraft is like Facebook."

"Facebook . . . ? Er, okay," I said. "Facebook."

It suddenly struck me that Facebook might be one of the alien inventions we were all using. I had seen its inventor on TV once and he definitely looked more alien than human.

"You have to be accepted as a friend before you get access. So stick your thumb in there."

She pointed at the part of the display that looked like an orange lightbulb, and I poked my thumb in. I didn't feel a thing, but the lightbulb turned sky-blue. Then Sonya did the same, and the bulb turned back to orange.

"Okay," she said. "You're in. From now on – *if* I let you take over the controls – all you'll have to do is grab the steering column and the Eggcraft will interpret everything else from your thoughts – safety protocols allowing, of course."

"You mean," I said, "I can fly this with my mind, and the Eggcraft will make sure I don't crash?"

"She'll do her best," Sonya said. "But don't push your luck. And don't let your mind wander. She'll get confused."

"Got it," I said, my mind already wandering, completely amazed by this incredible alien technology. Sonya did the wavy-hand thing again and suddenly we were airborne, hovering above the scrapyard about twenty feet off from the ground.

"Lesson two," she said. "People who stay alive fly Eggcraft with the cloaking device switched . . . "

I couldn't believe we were flying. In. A. Spaceship! I just wished my mom could see this.

Sonya cleared her throat.

Stared at me.

Rolled her eyes.

"*Oh* . . . I see, sorry," I said. "Er . . . cloaking device . . . on?"

"Brilliant," Sonya said. "It's that switch. Do it."

She pointed at the part of the holographic display that looked like three red doughnuts of top of one another. I ran my hand through it, and the doughnuts turned green.

"Eggcraft's completely civilian; no shields, no weapons," Sonya explained. "Without the cloaking device, we'd be sitting on ducks."

"Okay," I said. "But I think you mean 'we'd be sitting ducks'."

"Oh," she said. "Is that a sport here too?"

"I'm sure it is," I guessed. "Somewhere."

"You fleshies are one strange species," said Sonya. "But back to your lesson. You have to let your mind do the flying. Visualize where you want to go, how fast, and the Eggcraft computers will do your bidding. It's fly-by-mind."

"Great," I said, telling myself there was no way NATO could ever confuse this flying egg with the "rockets" I was banned from touching. "Can I launch us?"

"Who's the pilot?"

I pointed at her.

"Then watch and learn," she said with a smile. "And wait to be *invited*."

*   *   *

It wasn't until we reached the coast of California – night-flying over Los Angeles, *millions* of orange streetlights glowing in the gray night sky – that I finally got the controls.

At first, I was nervous, trying to keep my mind focused and clear of distractions, but the feeling was so all-encompassing that I didn't even want to think of anything else. I was consumed by the sensation of flying. It felt like magic, but of course I knew it was science, alien science. And for a rocket-savant like me, that made it all the more magical.

I willed the Eggcraft to buzz over the Hollywood sign and then flew out to the Pacific coast. I experimented with some Santa Monica wave-skimming, a few banking curves and some swooping dives. It was exhilarating.

There was a *tap tap tap* at the hatch.

"If you do that again," Octo called from the cabin, "I'll make sure it's *you* I throw up on!"

"You better not have spewed octo-puke on my crushed velvet!" said Sonya, leaving me in control as she disappeared into the cabin to check on her upholstery.

It was time to focus on the task at hand. I eased up on the steering column, kept my mind focused and clear, and settled into a smooth, coastal course towards Costa Rica, to the Monteverde Cloud Forest, for what Sonya had promised would be a perfect view of the active Arenal volcano.

"We need to get there ASAP," Sonya said, strapping herself back into the pilot's seat, but letting me stay at the controls. "Octo puked on NED and he's threatening to drain Octo's planet."

"What *is* it with NED?" I said. "Why's he such a jerk? And why would a guy who acts like a comic book super-villain walk around with such a lame name?"

"It's not *Ned*, dummy," Sonya explained. "It's N-E-D – stands for Non-Earth Deity. They're an entire *species* of minor deities, each member claiming dominion over a planet or two."

"You'd think his parents could afford private school," I said.

"He's been kicked out of most of them," she said, shaking her head. "I heard that his parents grounded him at Groom Lake to teach him some humility – trying to make him a more generous deity or something like that. But I'm sure they just wanted him out of their plasticky hair."

"Why's he got such a hold on you?"

"My planet worships the NEDs," she sighed. "We have this ancient tradition where the NEDs can summon any Aristox clan to perform this stupid ritual, a kind of musical dance—"

"The Balleropera?" I asked, remembering it from my first encounter with Sonya.

"That's it. I mean, on its own, it's actually a gorgeous

expression of life and self and art," she explained. "But in service of the NEDs, where just getting one move wrong is a capital crime, it's a disgusting reminder of Aristox subservience."

"Subservience like my dad making me polish his boots. He calls it character-building, but I call it child labor."

"Exactly like that," she said, "if the penalty for missing one speck of shine was . . . death."

"Gotcha," I said, even though I didn't fully understand how one species could willingly be subservient to another. "I'm glad I only get death *stares* from Dad."

"It's a good thing the Icons keep the NEDs cornered to one unlucky realm of the universe. The bad thing is that it just happens to include my planet."

"Icons like Juliet?" I said, my mind wandering to her unmatched blue beauty.

The Eggraft lurched starboard and plummeted in a downward spin.

"Get that blue chick out of your head!" Sonya shouted. "And focus on the flying!"

I shook myself out of the daydream, doing my best to banish all thoughts of the beautiful being from my head. I flew the egg steady with my newly clear mind, cruising at 800 mph.

"You'd better get in line, Romeo," Sonya huffed. "What is it with you boys?"

"Sorry."

"But at least she's a real deity. The Icons are wise, spiritual, compassionate, all-powerful, and they keep the NEDs in their place."

"So Juliet's all right?" I asked.

We tilted sharply to the port side. *Oops.*

Sonya punched my arm, Jessica-style. I straightened the Eggcraft for a second time.

"Look out the *window*, scaleless," Sonya said. "We're here. Put us down. Right there in that clearing."

As I guided the Eggcraft down among the trees, I suddenly knew why E.T.'s friends took so long to rescue him.

Spaceships are actually really hard to park.

CHAPTER FOURTEEN

Close Encounters of
the Magma Kind

The Costa Rican night sky was deep black, ash blotting out the stars. The only light came from the jagged, orange-glowing rivers – like liquid lightning – flowing down the dark slope of the volcano.

The five of us crouched in the darkness – the Eggcraft safely invisible farther up the ridge – in an earthy-smelling clearing in the middle of the cloud forest.

Maybe it was the fresh air, but for the first time, NED suddenly seemed *nice*. "Can't we . . . would it be . . . " he started. "Can we get a little bit closer? I think that would be *wonderful*."

"Nope," Sonya said. "There are tourists down there. Buses. Campsites. All packed with potential heart attacks at the sight of an android or a ventitent or an Aristox or a NED."

"Or a Sherman," said Octo, slapping me on the back. "He's no oil painting, either."

"Well ... " NED mused. "In that case ... what I might do is ... I think I'll ... "

With a sprint, he was gone. The trees and bushes shook as NED zipped through the jungle, heading for the volcano.

"Oh, great," Sonya said. "We're going to get busted."

"He looks human ... ish," I said. "Just a shame he'll be back for his ride home."

Now that NED had left us in peace, we took in the majestic sight of the Earth's core slowly rippling down the volcano.

"I hate to spoil the mood, people," Octo said after a few minutes. "But, Houston, are you taking any pics?"

"I'm recording it all," he said, sounding downhearted. The robot's mood seemed to have switched from negative to nostalgic.

"It's a pretty cool planet you've got here, Sherman," Octo said.

"It's home," I said, thinking about all of the Earth's wonders as viewed by alien visitors. Octo was right, and there was so much of my planet I'd yet to see. With my head almost permanently in the stars, had I been missing out on the wonders on the ground? "I guess we kinda take it for granted."

"At least you have a planet to call home," Houston said, solemnly.

"What do you mean?" asked Sonya.

"My planet is gone," he admitted. "That's why I'm here, on Earth. I've got nowhere else to go."

But before I could ask what had happened, a loud shriek pierced the night. It was NED, shouting at the top of his lungs.

"We'd better get him before he gets us into trouble," said Sonya.

We piled back into the Eggcraft and Sonya quickly guided the ship further up the vast volcano.

"He's up ahead," said Houston, tracking him on his built-in sonar system. Sonya hovered the Eggcraft just inches above the scorching river, where NED – singing and shouting like a mad man – was playing with, bathing in, then slurping up, hot lava.

I couldn't believe he wasn't burning, but NED was definitely fired up about something.

He scooped up the liquid magma like he was wading in a river of chocolate. In between gulps, NED blurted out, "Hints of cherry . . . an after-note of clove . . . what a *sensation*!"

"What's he doing? He's acting like my Uncle Charlie on New Year's Eve," I said. "I think he's . . . *drunk*!"

"Octo, can you grab him?" Sonya asked.

Octo opened the back hatch, dangled out his tentacles and wrapped them around the flailing NED.

Szzzzzz. Octo's skin sizzled where the lava splashed him.

"Ouch! Fried calamari was not meant to be on the menu tonight!" he cried.

"Do you have him?" asked Sonya.

Octo's burning tentacles pulled NED inside. He was tipsy and delirious, and I grabbed onto him. As much as I didn't like NED, I still didn't want him to fall out of the Eggcraft. Fortunately he was cool to the touch.

"I've got him!" I shouted, noticing that unlike the charred Octo, NED had no burn marks on him at all from the boiling lava. Strange.

The rear hatch finally sealed shut. I shoved NED onto the velvet bench and buckled him in. He keeled over, and then began blabbering into his neon phone:

"That's what I'm telling you, Dad," he said. "Yes . . . the whole planet *core* . . . yes . . . of *course* I tried some, it was *exquisite* . . . feeling a bit *woozy* though . . . you really ought to—"

"Ouchie-ouchie-ouch!" cried Octo. One of his tentacles was on fire.

I instinctively grabbed two of the flower vases from

the tables and doused his flaming appendage with water.

"*AHHHH!*" Octo cried. "*CHOOOOOOOOO!*"

The gigantic sneeze blew me into the cockpit, between Sonya and Houston.

I stayed put, safe for the moment, and tried to shake off the three beaks' worth of sticky snizz I'd been covered in, flicking boogers off my arms and legs.

"Sherman, no!" called Sonya.

I thought I'd accidentally tossed a booger her way, but when I climbed down from the dashboard to crouch between the two pilot seats, I realized I'd done something much, much worse.

"You deactivated the doughnuts!" cried Sonya. "We're not invisible!"

"Need the cream, need the cream," groaned Octo from the back. I remembered the first time I'd met Octo, in the nurse's office. Nurse Anderson had said something about special cream. "It's in my truck. Argh, hurts so much!"

I stared at Sonya and Houston, feeling panic rise in my chest. With Octo flambéed and NED as drunk as a skunk, we had to get home fast, but with the cloaking mechanism disabled, we were, as they say in the sporting world, sitting on ducks.

CHAPTER FIFTEEN

Outrunning the Air Force

While Sonya tried to reboot the cloaking mechanism, I'd taken Houston's place in the cockpit and was racing us north towards Groom Lake.

"Unidentified craft, do not attempt to enter United States airspace. Identify yourself or you will be fired upon."

The warning rang through the ship as we approached the southern US border.

"How long until we go invisible?" I asked.

"I don't know," said Sonya, fiddling with the wires and exposed computer components under the dashboard. "I bought the cloaker off eBay. It didn't come with a manual."

"Unidentified craft, if you enter United States airspace you will be fired upon. We have weapons locked."

I flinched as two fighter jets descended from above, flanking us closely.

"Your Air Force are a bit serious, aren't they?" said Sonya.

"You haven't meet my father, have you?" I said, thinking of my dad, a once four-star Air Force general turned chief stationery officer.

For a second, I actually considered phoning Dad to ask him to call off the impending air strike. But even if he did believe me, I was guilty of breaking two of his rules and as we were rapidly approaching nine o'clock, I was about to go for the hat-trick. He'd ground me for infinity. And while this airborne egg wasn't technically a *rocket*, I didn't want to take the chance that NATO would overlook the semantics and hand me over to the Russians as soon as we landed. No, we were on our own and I had to outrun the greatest Air Force on the planet.

"Unidentified craft, we have weapons locked – repeat, we have weapons locked – and will fire unless you leave United States airspace immediately, do you copy?"

"AHHHHHH," came a deep bellow from the cabin. Octo was clearly in pain. "Water hurts more than fire!"

"I say we turn back," urged Houston. "Expulsion is preferable to destruction."

"Very preferable," I said. "But Octo needs medical attention. Maybe I can reply to that warning?"

"Reply?" Sonya said. "With what? I don't even know how we're *hearing* them!"

"What?!" I said. "We're hearing them through your radio, aren't we?"

"Nope," she said. "I've got mp3 in here, but no radio. Seriously, who listens to the radio?"

"Unidentified craft, we have weapons locked – repeat, we have weapons locked – and will fire unless you leave United States airspace immediately, do you copy?"

"No *radio*?" I shouted. "What *is* this thing, just some kind of space *go-kart*?"

"Watch it, co-pilot."

I heard another groan from the cabin as Octo nursed his wounds.

"You okay back there, big guy?" I asked.

"NED's passed out and I'm in a world of pain," he grumbled. "So yeah, we're just peachy."

"It seems," Houston announced, "I have been acting as a radio receiver and audio amplifier."

"Oh, well . . . good," I said. "So *you* can reply, right?"

"Nope," Houston said.

"Even *you* don't have radio?" I said.

"I don't have that app."

"Unidentified craft, we have weapons locked – repeat, we

have weapons locked – and will fire unless you leave United States airspace immediately."

"How about GPS?" I asked.

"Of course, it's standard."

"Good, show me where we are."

Houston immediately projected a 3D, holographic map of the American southwest from his eyes onto the dashboard. I found what I was looking for. A great big hole in the middle of the landscape.

The Grand Canyon.

"There! We're going to lose them in there," I said, pushing the steering column forward and dropping us into a steep dive. I gave the Eggcraft all of the speed I could and zoomed down towards the scar in the Earth. I'd seen Will Smith do this in *Independence Day*, fleeing from alien fighter craft in his F-18. And if it was good enough for Will, it was good enough for Sherman. Of course, the roles were reversed and I was the one piloting an alien spacecraft, fleeing from the F-18s. I just hoped those pilots hadn't seen the movie.

I focused my mind and weaved us through the crevices. Even though it was night, Sonya's windshield digitally illuminated every rock of the canyon. I had perfect visibility.

Suddenly the entire Eggcraft pulsed red.

"They're firing on us!" Sonya shouted.

"Can't say they didn't warn us," Houston said.

I put us into a controlled spiral as a missile slammed into the rock wall above. Chunks of America's greatest natural wonder rained down on the Eggcraft, but the organic shell held up well.

"Aren't you glad I checked the hull before take-off?" quipped Houston.

I was.

"Bongo!" shouted Sonya.

"I don't think this is the time for music," I said, banking into a tight curve.

"No, bongo! I've done it, I've fixed the cloaker," she said, coming up from under the dashboard and taking the seat beside me.

"You mean *bingo*?"

"If you say so," she said. "But either way, we're invisible now. Let's get our patients back to base."

"Need the cream," called Octo again. "It's in my truck! Oh, sweet, soothing cream."

"I'll get you there as fast as I can," I said.

I swung us up out of the canyon, the F-18s still zooming through the dark crevices below, searching for a target that had just disappeared from their radar. I wondered how they were going to explain our disappearance to their superiors. Maybe we'd add to the UFO conspiracy theory? I liked the idea of being the only human in the canon of alien sightings.

I hung a left and flew us as fast as possible back to base, following Houston's GPS projection.

We zipped across southern Nevada to Groom Lake. The night was clear and, above the desert, a million stars sparkled in the sky. It was an amazing view, and for just a moment, I thought of Mom. I'd programed her rocket to release her ashes once the rocket hit sixty thousand feet. I knew it wasn't actually her, but I smiled to myself in the knowledge that little specks of her DNA were orbiting Earth, between the planet and those brilliant stars.

My wandering mind had drifted the Eggcraft skyward, and I refocused to regain control. Within minutes I had lowered the Eggcraft back down in the scrapyard, to the exact spot we'd departed from.

"That was mighty good flying, co-pilot," said Sonya.

"Thanks," I said. "It felt good."

And it did.

As I loosened my grip on the steering column, I let out a big sigh. It wasn't just relief, but something more: satisfaction. I only wished Dad could have seen how well I'd flown. I'd never wanted to follow in his footsteps as a pilot but, still, I was pretty impressed with myself.

"Ooooooh," purred Octo from outside, having raced to his truck the second we'd touched down. NED had come to when we'd landed then stumbled off looking dizzy, with no word of thanks for the trip.

I squeezed out of the cockpit and spotted his phone wedged into the cushions of his seat. I pocketed it, making a mental note to give it back to him tomorrow. I stepped down the Eggcraft's gangplank behind Houston, and found Octo scooping up purple cream from a barrel in his truck, lathering it all over his injured tentacle.

"Feeling better?"

"Much," he said, taking another scoop and rubbing it in. "Ooh, yeah, that tingling sensation means it's working!"

"Sorry about not getting that fire out faster," I said.

"Flames ain't fun, but water's worse," he said. "I'm allergic to it."

"That must be inconvenient," I said. "On a planet seventy per cent covered in the stuff."

"Thirty per cent dry land is more than enough for me. Can you check – have I missed a spot?"

I shook my head. "You're good."

"Then let's see those holo-photos, Metal Man!"

As Sonya used the remote keyring to lock the

Eggcraft, Octo led us into an empty hangar next to the office buildings where Houston could project the images he had taken of the volcano. Yes, we'd had an eventful night, but we still had a Planetology presentation to prepare for.

I marveled at how real the images looked as Houston flashed them onto a giant white metal wall.

Brrrr. Brrrr. Brrrr.

My pocket was vibrating.

"I think NED's got a text," I said, grabbing the phone from my pocket and reading the message aloud:

GR8 WORK, NED! YUM, YUM! EXTRACTION IN
8 WKS. DAD.
P.S. YOU'VE EARNED YOURSELF A PAIRING.
CHOOSE A HOTTIE!

Houston shuddered and the volcanic images vanished. "Did you say *Extraction*?" he asked.

"Yeah – what does it mean?"

We all leaned in to hear the answer.

"The end of the world," said Houston.

CHAPTER SIXTEEN

NEDageddon

I suddenly remembered NED's phonecall blabberings about magma being delicious and there being plenty of it. I started to get a very, very bad feeling.

"What do you mean, the *end* of the world?" I asked.

Houston's eyes lit up, literally. On the corrugated metal walls of the hangar, he projected images of green countryside, endless blue sky, oceans and shimmering silver cityscapes.

"Not the National Geographic Channel," complained Octo. "See if there's any boxing on?"

"It's stunning," I said.

"I haven't shown anybody these until now," Houston said, "but I think you need to know. This is . . . *was* . . . my world."

At first I thought they were images of Earth. But then trains started floating over tracks and airplanes with six wings flew across the sky. And then the people.

They weren't people at all. They were humanoid – one head, two arms and two legs – but they were stick-skinny, with pulsing skin in hues of rose, purple and green. I wondered if this was what Houston looked like underneath the metal.

"This is the visual archive of the planet Yaarian. My home."

The walls flickered with thousands more images. In silence, we watched these beings live, work, love and play; generation after generation. It was a breathtakingly beautiful and peaceful world, full of happy creatures with families, hopes and dreams.

"It's . . . perfect," Sonya said.

"It *was*," replied Houston, "until a giant ship arrived and drilled into our planet. We were given no warning, no time to evacuate. It efficiently sucked out Yaarian's magma core. When our leaders tried to negotiate with the ship, to plead with it to stop, all they got was a pre-recorded announcement: *We apologize for the inconvenience to your life, but the extraction process will be over soon.*

"There was nothing we could do to stop the ship draining every drop of magma from our planet's core. They called it extraction, but we called it *extinction*."

We were silent with sympathy, not knowing what to say – and then Houston continued.

"My parents knew the end was near and wanted to save my . . . me. And so they digitized me. I gave up my organic body and woke up in this ecto-shell, a kind of robotic lifeboat. Just seconds before my world collapsed in on itself, they launched me to a faraway world called Earth. I was the only survivor."

We watched as images of a burning, collapsed world flashed onto the walls, the terror and suffering of the beings clear. Then the images faded, and Houston hung his head.

"I'm so sorry, Houston," said Sonya, wiping back a tear. "I had no idea."

Octo gave Houston a tentacle hug.

"It must've been the NEDs and I think they're going to do it again," whispered Houston from within Octo's embrace. "To Earth."

And then NED's phone rang.

"Hello?" I said, pressing the button I guessed was speakerphone.

"*Sher*-man?" said NED. "You are about to seriously regret stealing my phone."

"Listen, NED, we're not going to let you—"

Sonya slapped the phone from my palm. It skidded across the dusty floor, crackled like a sparkler and exploded. Pieces sizzled, just like our planet was going to do.

"We have to warn everyone!" I said.

"But NED just destroyed the evidence," said Sonya, pointing to the pieces of phone.

"I'll talk to my dad," I said. "He can warn the authorities, the Air Force, the entire military!"

"When the extraction starts," said Houston, "there's nothing your Earth authorities can do to stop it."

I'd had a lot of bad first days of school, but this took the cosmic cake. I'd stumbled upon a plot to destroy the world. My head spun as the text message flickered in my memory: EXTRACTION IN 8 WKS.

And Houston's words haunted me.

They called it extraction. We called it extinction.

★　★　★

I found Jess in the kitchen finishing her English homework, a short essay on the ethnocentric bias of author H.G. Wells. I asked her where Dad was.

"Everyone on the base got called in," she said. "He said something about a UFO sighting."

"And what, they need more envelopes?"

"I don't know, Sherman, but he'd just sat down to watch football when this siren-thing blasted out and suddenly Dad and all the other grown-ups had to go into work. Didn't you hear it?"

"Um, yeah," I lied. "But we were pretty focused on the Planetology stuff."

Jessica returned to her essay and I waited up for Dad in the living room, surfing the off-world channels on satellite. I flicked through xenophile soap operas (everybody was totally cheating on everybody), AJABot crime capers (some pretty graphic robot dismemberment) and a Yazzerbeast reality show called *Eat It or Feed It?* (to which I must admit the safest answer is *neither*).

I must've fallen asleep because the next thing I knew Dad was stirring me awake on the sofa. I had a lingering sense that I may have been dreaming about doing the balcony scene with Juliet. Naked.

"Come on, kiddo," he said. "Off to bed."

"Dad, Jess said there was a UFO tonight," I began.

"That's classified, Sherman," he said. "But yes, something appeared in our airspace and then just . . . disappeared. Around here I've learned that *unidentified* means *paperwork*, and paperwork means more work for the Stationery Officer."

I sat up on the Air-Force-issue beige sofa and tried to convince him that I was a *bona fide* prophet of Armageddon.

"Dad, it's more than that. There's an alien invasion coming, and it's going to destroy the world."

"You were probably dreaming," he said. "You were mumbling about killing an envious moon."

"I wasn't," I said, not being entirely truthful. There was no way I'd tell Dad about the naked balcony scene. "I, I can't tell you how I know, but I know. It's the NEDs. They're going to suck the magma out of the Earth's core, and it'll destroy the planet!"

"Sherman, is this a cry for help?"

"No," I said, "well, yes, I guess. Yes, I need your help. To stop it."

"Son, the Bureau has extensive peace treaties with all of the aliens here, including the NEDs. It's a delicate diplomatic puzzle of alien relations, and the last thing we need is to be making serious accusations about a peaceful ally. Because if there's one thing aside from rockets that you should avoid, it's causing a diplomatic incident."

"But, Dad, they're not peaceful! NED's a bully and a jerk and he—"

"Are you being bullied at school, Sherman?"

How was I supposed to answer that one?

I'd been suspended over a garbage can by a teenage yeti and endured the scowls and slurs of a plastic low-ranking deity, but I didn't want to distract Dad from the big issue.

"No, Dad, but you have to listen. The invasion is coming and we only have—"

"When I was your age," he said, "my parents sent me to military school and it was the best thing that happened to me. Taught me discipline, moral fortitude, and kept me grounded in reality."

"This *is* real, Dad," I pleaded. "The NEDs are going to suck out the Earth's core just like they did to Houston's planet. NED tasted the volcano tonight and he—"

"Did you just say volcano?"

"Maybe. Why?" I realized I'd said too much.

"We had reports about the same UFO hovering over a volcano in Costa Rica. The Bureau's fending off every agency in the government tonight." He rhymed them off like a jumbled-up alphabet. "INS. CDC. ATF. FBI. CIA. IRS. Even the UN weapons inspectors want a look-in! All because a suspicious UFO turned up in Costa Rica. Costa Rica, Sherman. As in, a very long way away. As in, so far away that if any students were there tonight in an unauthorized departure from this base, it would lead to more than a serious grounding. Now, you don't know anything about that, do you?"

"Um, no," I said.

"Good answer. Now off to bed, leave the poor moon alone and try to stay grounded in reality."

CHAPTER SEVENTEEN

Pastry High

Over the following week, I tried again and again to alert the adults to the impending doomsday, but Dad just wouldn't hear it.

It was hard to concentrate on school when I was certain the world was going to end, but the one highlight was rehearsing with Juliet. I was glad I could spend the last days of Planet Earth with her. She was magical. And it wasn't just her glow. Her smart, sweet and knowing presence was so incredible to be around that those terrible memories of life on Old MacDonald's Farm started to slip away. I was crushing on her in a serious way.

At school, I pretended everything was normal. But between classes and homework, I tried to conjure up a plan to save the world. We'd all tried to warn our parents. Sonya's folks refused to listen to her "blasphemous" talk And Octo's attempts to alert his folks fell on deaf ears, or at least whatever passed for ears in ventitent biology. "The NEDs are so regal and sophisticated," his mom had said.

"And generous," added his father. "They always send us that gift box just stuffed with chocolate-covered shrimp for the holidays."

With no parents of his own, Houston warned Principal Meltzer, only to receive a lecture about the dangers of spreading rumors. Nobody on base wanted to take us seriously. So, we would have to take matters into our own hands . . . and tentacles.

One day, right after Home Economics class, I had a revelation.

We were baking Rilperdough, a sentient pastry that acts like your favorite pet – rubbing itself up against you, begging for treats – but it looks, smells and feels like Play-Doh, bent into half-moons. It's one of the weirdest things I've seen at this school so far – *and* these space-faring croissants babble constantly in a language that sounds like high-pitched Italian in reverse.

But if there's one thing I've learned in Home Ec, it's not to sweat the baked stuff.

You just knead them and place them on a greaseproof tray, and put the whole gang in the oven at 350 degrees for twenty minutes.

Because translated, the reverse-Italian means one thing:

"Bake us!"

That's what our teacher, Mr Zvisst (who looked like wobbly cherry Jello and could divide himself into however many chefs a kitchen – or classroom – required) told us over and over as we kneaded our Rilperdough and sharpened our knives. "Rilperdough," he said, "heads for ovens the way salmon head upstream."

It's a lifecycle thing.

So once I knew we were helping the little guys out, kneading them into shape was pretty soothing. At least it gave me some time to think. If the adults of Groom Lake weren't going to save the world, maybe there was something Sherman Capote could do.

The *bleep bleep bleep* of my oven timer snapped me out of my daydream, so I grabbed my floral oven mitts and pulled open the oven door.

The smell was incredible.

Marzipan, cookie dough, a little cinnamon, but also hints of pine needle and something I couldn't quite place . . . Crazy Glue maybe.

We all clattered our trays onto our counters. The little baked aliens glowed. But it wasn't heat. It was something more ethereal.

Mr Zvisst had split himself into twelve smaller versions of himself, patrolling every counter, handing out plastic containers and reeling off instructions in perfect, tranquil unison.

"The Rilperdough are ready," Mr Zvisst cooed.

"So each cook's duty . . . "

" . . . is to ensure their desserts are consumed . . . "

" . . . within five minutes from now . . . "

" . . . before their glow fades . . . "

" . . . one consumer per Rilperdough . . . "

" . . . no second helpings . . . "

" . . . no second thoughts!"

I gently filled my plastic container, grabbed my stuff and joined the crowd squeezing through the sliding silver doors into the hallway, feeling a little anxious about the approaching rush to honor the freshly baked.

Not a great time to find myself side-by-side with NED (and side-by-shaggy-thigh with Graz). But then again, when is?

"I hear you've been saying things about me," he said, fixing me with a dark glare.

"I know what you're up to, NED, and I'm going to stop you."

"Oh, *Sher*-man, those are big words for a little man

who can't even stop his hair from frizzing," he laughed, gliding away down the hall.

I ran my hand over my head – he was right. My hair was practically on end. I tried to slap it down.

As I shimmied through a troop of bleeping AJABots and dodged an earthy-smelling gaggle of Fungi, I bumped into Jessica.

She was striding along the hallway in a black lace dress over ripped jeans. And she was talking a lot, pointing this way and that. Five Martians – the little gray guys in the jumpsuits with the big eyes – were following her, taking down her every word on transparent digital notepads.

"And seriously," she said, "if I see one balloon in these corridors, I'll flip. I'll flip dramatically, and I'll flip dangerously. Ribbons, not balloons. In school colors of course, and—"

"Jessica," I said, grabbing her and forcing the plastic container of Rilperdough into her hands. "You have to eat one of these."

"If you made this, Sherman," she said, "I'm not putting it in my mouth."

The little guys immediately understood what was in the container, took it gently from me and shared out the Rilperdough, one piece each.

"You have to, Jessica," I said. There was still one left over, as well as mine.

The Martians munched. They made contented *hmmmmmm* noises.

"Eat! Eat!" they said, once they'd swallowed. "The glow! The glow!"

Finally, Jessica took a small bite. And, astonishingly, she managed a kind-of smile.

"Not bad," she said, which was probably the closest thing to a compliment she could bring herself to give me. "We should serve this at Prom. Write that down!"

The Martians took the dictation and then gathered around me, pushing my Rilperdough towards my mouth.

"I'm the new chair of the Prom committee," Jessica announced, "and if you find some way to mess that up, I'll get you probed by aliens!"

"I may have already messed it up, Jess," I said. "The world is going to end."

"Don't write that down, Klaatu," Jessica said to the nearest Martian, who was busy putting pen to pad. "He's not on the committee."

I took a bite of my Rilperdough, and munched. The Crazy Glue fumes must have gone to my head, because suddenly I just didn't care.

"Very funny, Sherman," Jessica said, responding

to my end-of-the-world announcement. "And yet, the fact you would even *say* that, tells me so much about your *obvious* desire to ruin any happiness I may find for myself, no matter what I . . . "

As she blathered on, Jessica seemed to transform into a cartoon version of herself. I was blissed out by the Rilperdough filling my insides with joy. The moment I took a bite, I felt like I hadn't felt since I was about five. Watching jets take off with my dad when he still liked me, *Science Fiction Theatre* after my bath on Sunday nights, building my first rocket . . . and when Mom used to let me lick the icing off the mixer when she'd baked a birthday cake. The Rilperdough somehow unearthed all of my happiest memories and make me feel like they were happening again, right here, right now.

I wondered if that was how a deity like Juliet felt all of the time.

And that's when the idea came – as effortlessly as picking rocket parts from a scrapyard.

I realized that even if nobody was going to stop the NED invasion, there was one person on Earth more powerful than the NEDs. My Juliet!

"Jess, when is Prom?"

"Like you'll ever have a date to go with," she teased.

"*When?*"

"May the fourth," she said.

"Praise Lucas," uttered the Martians in unison.

I remembered the text message from NED's dad and did the math in my head. *Seven weeks away. Just in time.*

The plan took shape in my mind. Icons were more powerful than NEDs. So, if I could keep Juliet – an omnipotent deity – on Earth until the NED invasion, she could bodyguard the planet. Her mere presence would stop the extraction – the NEDs wouldn't dare do it with an Icon around. And the extraction was planned for the same day as the Prom. Suddenly it was so clear: Juliet had to be my date, you know, to save the world!

It was a daring idea, an idea of such stupefying *genius* that it needed an audience as soon as humanly, or *alienly*, possible.

As the Rilperdough wore off and cartoon-Jessica morphed back into real-life-Jessica, nattering on about Prom this and decorations that, I floated on a new-found cloud of confidence down the hall in search of my friends.

It was time for Sherman Capote to save the world.

I went straight to the packed cafeteria, collected my food and found Sonya, Octo and Houston at our very own lunch table.

"Nice to have real estate, huh?" said Octo, stuffing two of his beaks with burgers and fries. By now, word of our field trip had gone viral and we had what Octo liked to call "street cred".

"This is officially *our* table!" Octo continued.

"Too bad the world's going to end," Sonya said. She flicked her tongues, slurped her spearmint slushie and tapped a scaly, perfectly-manicured finger on the table. "It kind of puts a dampener on our social climbing."

"Don't worry," I said, tucking into my seafood lasagne. "I have a plan for that."

Octo looked at my plate. "You're probably eating my distant cousin right now. Are you really okay with that?"

I spluttered, put my knife and fork down – appetite well and truly lost – and announced my genius plan. "I'm going to save the world."

"Awesome," said Octo. "Pass the ketchup."

"How?" asked Sonya.

"Just pick it up and pass it over," the ventitent said impatiently.

"By taking Juliet to the Prom," I answered.

Houston tossed a bottle of the red stuff to Octo and the three of them stared at me.

"Okay," Octo mumbled. "It's . . . er . . . good to have goals." He tentacle-slapped me on the back.

"Lofty goals," added Sonya.

"And your *plan* is?" Houston said.

"That is the plan," I said. "Its brilliance is its simplicity!"

"Why do *you* have to take *Juliet* to the Prom?" Sonya asked.

"If she's here on Earth when the invasion comes," I explained, "she'll protect the planet against the NEDs. They won't dare carry out the extraction with her here."

"In theory, the logic holds," Houston announced. "But in practice, it's inherently flawed."

"What? No!" I said. "It's flawless."

"Yeah, metal-head," said Octo. "Why you gotta be a player-hater?"

"I'm with Houston on this," Sonya said, shaking her head. "Tell them why."

"Because Juliet is a breathtakingly attractive deity," Houston announced, "who could, quite literally, choose any guy in the universe. And Sherman is . . . well, Sherman."

The only thing that hurts more than the truth, is the truth as told by your friends.

"You're not exactly at the same . . . what's the word?" started Sonya.

"Table?" I said. "I know, I gotta close the gap but—"

"Standard," she said. "You're not exactly at the same standard as Juliet. She sits up there, literally and figuratively on a pedestal, and even though we've got our own table now – and yes, Octo, it's great to have real estate – let's face it, we're down here. Where we belong."

I suddenly realized just how Sonya's people were subjugated by the NEDs. They *allowed* themselves to be controlled by thinking they weren't good enough.

"No offence," she added, as if that suddenly made it all okay.

But she had a point. Why would Juliet give up a thousand amazing worlds filled with probably billions of cooler guys just to go to a stupid dance with me?

I didn't know, but I had to make it happen.

The fate of the planet depended, entirely, on my mojo.

Field of Pains

The next day in PE, I discovered the only thing worse than an impending magma-draining apocalypse: football.

Until Groom Lake, I'd only ever been to international schools, where football was a "beautiful game" that actually involved kicking a ball with your foot. Back in the States, however, they favored the bone-crushing Super Bowl version. I could just about hold my own running around after a black-and-white ball, but avoiding death by blind-side tackle was not my idea of a physical education.

The heat was unbearable under the supposedly protective pads, but it was the humiliation that really stung. My dad had been the star quarterback in his glory days, but I was about flying rockets, not throwing balls. Being a rocket man is an all-consuming vocation. It's a *calling*. And when your every thought's way up above the Kármán Line, it's pretty hard to care about who catches the pigskin on the ground. For me, football was just one giant reminder of a hundred fumbled catches in a dozen backyards, my dad shaking his head in disappointment and going back inside for a pastrami sandwich and some NFL on satellite.

On this particularly scorching Groom Lake afternoon, I was cast as a wide receiver. My motivation was apparently to catch the ball, but what really motivated me was staying alive on the field. Octo was the quarterback of my team and Houston the kicker. The girls were in the gym (in the air conditioning) playing basketball, so it was just us guys on the field. And testosterone (or whatever aliens have) was off its leash.

"Anyone I should watch out for?" I asked Octo, scanning the opposing team for threats.

"The giant scorpion," Octo whispered into my helmet, "definitely wants to pulverize you."

The scorpion was the line backer for the other team – a seven-foot mass of black, gnarly armor with a couple of claws the size of sofa cushions. He strutted around upright on his spindly hind claws and, instead of arcing his tail over his head, like the regular-sized Nevada-desert scorps do, he dragged it across the ground menacingly. I was keen to avoid him, but Octo was right: the scorp seemed to have it in for me.

And, just to spice things up, Coach Caan's phone rang (*"the Mrs again"*), and he put the scorpion in charge of the game.

"What if he *stings* me?" I asked.

"Your head will probably turn purple and swell until sweet death saves you from unimaginable agony," Octo answered cheerfully.

"But he'll likely be expelled," added Houston.

"Did we steal his lunch table or something?" I wondered.

"Like he'd let us," scoffed Octo.

"One of NED's henchmen maybe?"

"Nope," Octo said. "Varsity through and through. Superjock. Name's Atawee."

"Then *what*—?"

Atawee blew his whistle, threw it on the turf, spit, then banged his claws together.

"Lisssen up," he said with a slight hiss. "Run the play again. But thisss time, leave the new kid to me!"

Great. That meant when the AJABot playing center snapped the ball to Octo, and I ran downfield in a hopeless attempt to catch Octo's pass, it would be the interstellar killer scorpion with the mystery grudge and lethal stinger who tackled me.

"Ah, you'll be fine, Sherman," Octo said, lining up the scrimmage. "Just remember my advice."

I took my stance, preparing to die.

"TWENTY-SEVEN, FORTY-NINE ... " Octo called.

"Advice?" I yelled.

"Run faster than him," Octo said. "SEVENTY-TWO, THIRTY NINE ... "

The AJABot snapped the ball to Octo and I ran as fast as I could. Octo hurled a perfect spiral in my direction. As it soared, I wondered if Sonya's Eggcraft would be more aero-efficient if it spiraled like a football and whether—

SLAM!

Atawee hit me like a truck squishing a squirrel. He pinned me down and growled into my helmet (which I was pretty sure would have to be surgically removed).

"Heard about your airborne manoeuvresss, sssquishy," he hissed. "Outrunning the Air Force isn't easily done. Consider yourself recruited."

"Um, uh," I grunted. "For what?"

"Rocket Races. And I'm sssponsoring you. Don't. Let. Me. Down."

So he wasn't going to sting me, yet. For a full second, the world was undeniably a wonderful place again – but then reality sank in, and all I could think about were gulags. Dark, dangerous, death-bringing gulags.

"I'm really sorry," I said. "But I'm not your guy. I'll go to prison if I touch a rocket."

"That's your problem," Atawee whispered. "So unless you want to feel the sharp end of my stinger, I'd get yourself a crew together and get prepped. Trials are in five weeks."

"I'll think about it," I said, weighing up a sudden death by scorpion against a cruel, slow expiration in a gulag.

"Don't think too hard," he said, clicking his claw against my helmet. "You might hurt your head."

He sprang off me and resumed his stand-in coaching duties. Octo scooped me up, hauled me to the touchline, and checked my vitals.

"You'll live," he said. "Guess he didn't like the taste of you?"

"He wants to recruit me for the Rocket Races."

"That's huge!" Octo shouted.

"Yeah, a huge problem," I said. "He's going to kill me if I don't race, but I'm as good as dead if I do – you know I'm not allowed anywhere near rockets."

"Well, it's what I call a high-class problem," he said. "Look, only the cool kids compete in the Rocket Races.

And if you race, then you'll be cool too. Plus, it's a universal truth that chicks dig guys that go fast. It's a sure-fire way to impress Juliet."

I didn't want to argue with his logic, nor ask why he considered himself such an expert on human dating dynamics, because he did have a point. All of the fighter pilots I'd met had always had pretty wives or girlfriends.

"But if I'm caught racing, I'm toast. Maybe I should just get Juliet to like me for, well, *me*?"

Houston laughed, joining our huddle.

"Don't take this the wrong way," Octo said, hoisting me to my feet, "but you're no teen idol, and you're not exactly All American on the field. Dude, I hate to break it to you, but you are not exactly cool."

First Houston and Sonya, then Octo. Where was the loyalty?

"Octo, you're not *exactly* an authority on cool," I said, trying to keep my confidence.

"But I'm not trying to date a deity," he said. "For a guy like you to get a girl like Juliet – especially to get a girl like Juliet to the *Prom* – you've got only one option."

"Which is?" I asked.

"You've got to defy the terrifying odds and somehow *become* cool by being seen *doing* something cool way, way, way better than anyone else."

I slumped. He was right.

"And you, buckaroo," he said, "have just one skill set to draw on there."

"But if I'm going to race a rocket, I'm going to need a disguise," I said. "Something really good – that'll fool everyone, except for Juliet."

"I knew . . . *know* someone who can help there," offered Houston, cryptically. "I can get you a disguise."

Octo patted us both on our backs with his tentacles. "Then we meet at the hangar tonight, rocket men!"

CHAPTER NINETEEN

If You Build It

That night, during a spaghetti-and-meatballs dinner, Dad quizzed us half-heartedly on our days. Jess announced that in addition to becoming Prom committee chairperson, she was now editor of the yearbook.

"I even got invited to sit at the cool tables in the cafeteria, Dad," she gloated. "And that's like a really big deal."

She'd somehow managed to elevate her social status, right up to the rarefied tables along the wall. I couldn't believe it. My twin sister was now in the exclusive company of the cool seniors, the cool juniors and of course the cafeteria monitors. Without even knowing it, she was rubbing my distinct uncoolness in my face.

"I get to decide what is remembered about this year at Groom Lake," she bragged, turning to me, "and what is forgotten."

I sighed. Unless my plan worked, Jessica would be in charge of archiving our last days on Earth.

"Top-gun, Jessica! I'm very proud of the way you're fitting in here," Dad said, slurping spaghetti into his mouth. I almost laughed. With long strands of red pasta hanging from his mouth, he actually looked like an alien.

"Thanks, Dad," Jess said as she cut her pasta into little pieces. "I'm really starting to find my groove here."

"Enjoy it while it lasts," I said as I twirled. I've always been a twirler. When it comes to spaghetti, I seek to create order from the chaos on my plate. I twirled my spaghetti strands into an expertly-shaped cone of pasta around my fork, like the command module of the Apollo rockets. "It'll be great to have a yearbook commemorating Earth's last year of existence."

"Sherman Capote," snapped Dad. "You should be supportive of your sister, and you should be trying to fit in too."

"I played football today," I offered.

"Yeah," laughed Jess. "I heard he got crushed in a tackle. Heard your octopus friend had to scoop you off the thirty-yard line."

"That's great, Sherman," said Dad. "Football made me the man I am today."

"I thought that was military school?" I asked.

"Or the Air Force?" chimed Jess.

"Football was the foundation of all of that: focus, discipline and inner strength."

"Just like yearbook!" said Jess.

"Exactly," said Dad.

"And rocket-building," I said. "I used to get all of that from rocketeering."

"But football never almost-caused a world war, Sherman," Dad said.

"That's because it's an American-only sport," I said. "Nobody else cares."

"Sherman, sometimes you exasperate me."

★ ★ ★

After dinner I raced through my Math homework and then waited until Dad and Jess fell asleep to sneak out to meet Octo at the hangar next to the scrapyard. Sonya and Houston were there too. I smiled at them – I needed all the help I could get.

"So you're going to be a racer, eh?" asked Sonya.

"I figure it'll teach me focus, discipline and inner strength," I said.

"And get you the girl," added Octo.

"And save the planet," said Houston.

"That's the general idea," I said.

"Then we're your crew," Sonya announced, "and

we'd better get started. We've got a rocket to build and a racer to train."

We didn't waste any time. Octo and I scoured the scrapyard for usable rocket parts while Houston and Sonya separated and organized our haul into the essential categories: engines, fuselage, boosters and guidance.

We debated and discussed what type of racer to build.

"The fastest one possible," I said.

"But it's a trade-off between speed and maneuverability," explained Sonya.

"Speed, speed, speed!" shouted Octo.

"Agility and control," countered Houston.

The possibilities were mind-blowing: saucer, airplane style, bi-plane, tri-plane, X-Wing, Enterprise, or NASA-issue STS. We debated aerodynamics, torque and hovering capacity. I may have been banned from Rocket Camp, but out here, at night, I was getting a full education on the galaxy's best space technology. It was the first time I'd had friends to talk about rockets with. I guessed this was how normal people felt in football teams, chess clubs and choirs: like they belonged.

Unlike our competitors, whom Sonya said would stick to their own kinds as single-species crews, we had four different planets' worth of know-how to pull from. So we were going to put our diversity to our advantage.

As we talked, Houston projected a constantly updating 3D hologram of what we were proposing. Slowly, a model took form.

We agreed to combine the speed of a missile-style rocket with the maneuverability of Sonya's Eggcraft. Houston illustrated a fusion-powered double-rocket chassis with a crew cabin on top, fronted by the nose of a modified F-18.

Somewhere, Will Smith was smiling.

★ ★ ★

Every night, when the melting pot of Groom Lake went to sleep, we met up at the hangar to build our racer. It was like having two lives. During the day, we'd go through the motions of school life – classes, lunches, bully avoidance – and at night, we'd meet to make the ship of our dreams.

Despite Houston's promise of a disguise for the races, I was still fearful of getting caught. But one night, as the schematics for the racer were coming together, he wheeled in a large steel trunk.

He opened the lid, revealing his solution. "This is how your identity will be hidden from the authorities."

I gasped when Houston opened the box. His own severed head stared back at me from inside. It was tucked away with a dismembered metal torso and and four limbs. The case housed a Houston doppelganger. Brand new, some assembly required.

"Someone you know?" asked Sonya, tentatively.

"Not all of my people successfully made the transition to robot form. This ecto-shell was for my . . . is vacant," said Houston.

Octo put one tentacle round Houston's shoulders, another around mine.

"So who," I asked, "was this suit meant for, you know, originally?"

"My twin brother, Aldrin," Houston said. "He didn't survive the digitization process."

We went quiet for a little while. I didn't know what to say. Jessica was annoying but there was a comfort in being a twin. I couldn't imagine losing that. I thought of Buzz Aldrin and how Houston's parents must have heard about – or seen – the human moon landings, just like my parents did, all those decades ago.

"But if anybody asks," he continued, "I'll say that you arc him, Sherman. It's only fitting, he *was* named after a brave human rocketeer."

"Houston, it'll be an honor," I said, shaking his hand. "I'll be sure to do your brother proud."

CHAPTER TWENTY

School Days and Rocket Nights

The one class I'd always loathed before moving to Groom Lake was fast becoming a firm favorite. Drama was a lot more fun when you were the leading man. Octo was cast as Mercutio, Romeo's ill-fated best friend, and a Yazzerbeast named Crezzert was typecast as Tybalt. In art imitating life, Romeo also had an unsupportive father, to be played by a Martian called Quudo.

I was starting to master the Shakespearean dialogue and loved every scene with Juliet. I don't know if it was my crush, the fact that human survival depended on my wooing her, or her otherworldly acting skills, but when we were on stage, I was convinced that we were destined to be together.

When we rehearsed Act One, Scene Five, Romeo and Juliet's first meeting, the energy was electric. I got to lean in and kiss her for the first time – *Then move not, while my prayer's effect I take* – and my lips literally sizzled. It felt like a small fraction of the power of the universe passed between us. It was energizing and alien at the same time.

And I wasn't the only one who seemed to be crushing. A natural pairing-off had occurred in our little rocket crew. While Octo had moved into my never-before-occupied best friend position, even inviting me over to his tank for dinner, Houston and Sonya became a dynamic duo. At the hangar, they were completely in sync, passing each other the right tools without so much as a word between them. And when they did talk, they finished each other's sentences.

"Is there something going on between you and Sonya?" I asked Houston one night, my curiosity getting the better of me.

"No – we're just friends, and work well together and . . . " He looked round to check that she wasn't close by. "Why, do you think she likes me?"

"You guys seem pretty tight," I said.

"Is that a good thing on this planet?"

I smiled. I was glad I wasn't the only one embarking on an interplanetary, cross-cultural romance. Romeo and Juliet may have had warring families keeping them apart, but Juliet and I, Houston and Sonya; we had intergalactic culture to overcome.

* * *

One night, after an intense session assembling the cockpit, I crept back to the hangar because I'd forgotten my backpack. But I wasn't alone.

As I rounded the corner I heard footsteps, one set soft, the other heavy. At first, I was scared our secret assembly space had been discovered, but as I ducked behind the nearest stack of pallets to see who was there, I spotted Sonya and Houston.

Dancing.

Sonya soared with graceful jumps that were a complete mismatch to the black overalls she was wearing.

And Houston wasn't just following her lead, he was stalking her. Just a couple of paces behind. Never taking his eyes off her for a second . . .

It wasn't until he projected a floating image of Sonya dancing that I realized he was filming her, recording and playing it back in full 3D holographic glory.

He was helping her to practice the Balleropera, the ritual dance her species performed for the NEDs.

I watched in secret for over an hour – being tucked

away watching my friend practice an amazing array of jumps, lunges and vocal acrobatics was a pretty good night's entertainment.

I smiled, but it was only a small smile. Sonya looked so happy dancing with Houston. I just wished the dance didn't come with the death penalty.

CHAPTER TWENTY-ONE

Meet the Octos

One night, I followed Octo's tentacle-drawn map to a warehouse five blocks from our secret hangar to finally meet his folks. Their home was actually about the same size as the hangar, only much newer and shinier. When the massive iron door rumbled open I half-expected to see a stealth bomber inside. But instead, my twenty-tentacled friend glided out of the darkness.

"Welcome to the aquarium," Octo said. "My folks can't wait to meet you."

After the blazing early-evening sunshine, the darkness of Octo's pad seemed pitch black (though beautifully cool and air-conditioned). But though my eyes adjusted to the Sea World-sized alien aquarium, my brain pretty much refused to.

I was surrounded by an enormous U-shaped tank, home to two massive ventitents. Octo's mama and papa were as big as killer whales. Octo was a miniature carbon copy of his dad, but his mom had purple tiger-stripes instead of yellow, and – I *think* – some equivalent of lipstick on her beaks, because they were a glossy ruby-red. Or was it crimson? It was hard to tell with the green hue of the water.

Little galaxies of bubbles swirled upwards every time they moved. Somewhat disturbingly, I could hear their hearts beating – rhythmic, pounding, underwater drums.

"Mom, Dad," Octo said, "*this* is Sherman. Sherman, this is my mom, Urta, and my dad, Hank."

Octo sat me at the head of the table that was surrounded by the U-shaped tank, and he squatted opposite. Hank and Urta floated in the water beside us with their tentacles intertwined lovingly.

"Good afternoon, sir, ma'am," I said. "Thanks for having me over. Oh, and my dad says to say, great work with the recovery in the Pacific."

A small, orange-cuboid robot with telescopic arms hovered out of the darkness and poured cans of Pepsi into the glasses of ice by our plates.

"That was an adventure," chuckled Urta.

"And romantic," added Octo's dad in a gurgling, baritone-deep voice, which I suddenly realized I could hear from little loudspeakers on the rim of the aquarium.

"We spent a few days off the coast of Hawaii after that mission, just the two of us."

Urta swam towards the glass. "Word in the BAA community is that your father's doing a bang-up job in Stationery."

"Um, yeah," I said. "I don't think he's loving pushing envelopes."

"We all do our bit, Sherman," said Hank.

"I suppose you're right," I said, thinking aloud. "All these aliens, living here, but doing their best to stop the human race from freaking out at not being the only intelligent species in the universe. I guess it's a lot of work, right? Work that requires deep sea recovery and a steady stream of stationery."

"He's certainly intelligent," said Urta, smiling with all three rouged beaks. Octo's dad looked down at Octo with what I could only interpret as an approving nod.

"You're right, son," came a bellow from the loudspeaker. "He *is* smarter than he looks."

The top of the tank was completely open. A fluorescent green lagoon. Little waterfalls cascaded from pipes at the corners, and every so often tentacle-tips flicked above the surface like a Loch Ness monster sighting.

The Z-Five robot served up pizza-sized crispy green leaves onto our table, then leaped into the tank and delivered pincerfuls of the stuff to Hank and Urta.

"Let's eat," Octo said.

"Deep-fried Phaxxosian sea moss," Hank said, munching. "We get it imported from the deli on U'hoa 3, where we first met. Isn't that right, my lovely?"

Urta planted a kiss on Hank's cheek. "When it was just the two of us," she said. "And now our little boy is all grown up."

She turned to Octo and said, "Oh, how we've missed you."

It turned out Octo had been home alone – or rather, *squidysat* by the robot – for a few weeks. Hank and Urta worked with the Salvage and Rescue Division of the Bureau, and had just helped raise a crashed Xentaurian mothership from the bottom of the Pacific.

"You should have seen it, Sherman," Hank said. "Imagine a skyscraper bursting up from the ocean . . . "

"Was anyone on board still alive?" I asked.

"That ship is thirty-two thousand years old," said Urta. "So, no, dear."

"But the interesting thing is that about that same time the Xentaurians' home planet was being destroyed by a geological event," added Hank in classic, dad-knows-best tone of voice.

I looked at Octo and mouthed, *NEDs?*

Octo nodded, mouthing, *Has to be.*

"Think about it, Sherman," Hank continued. "The surface of this little world of yours, it's blue. Seventy per cent water. Most of what crashes here ends up on the seabed, and some of it's been there a long, long time."

Hank and Urta told some great stories about deep diving, salvaging alien relics and even rescuing a ship full of teenagers who'd crashed in the Arctic from Xelian9. Unlike my dad, these two clearly loved their jobs with the Bureau.

"But never mind all that," Urta declared. "What really matters is this sister of yours. Octo's quite besotted."

"Be-what?" I teased. "Oh, you mean he's totally crushing on the swamp monster I'm forced to live with?"

"Ooh, she's from a swamp, is she?" asked Urta. "Good breeding eggs, those swamp monsters, I'll have you know."

Octo's yellow stripes turned bright pink and he rolled his eyes at me. "See what you started."

His folks giggled with the gentle, teasing laughter of a sitcom family. It was the kind of laugh-track that had been absent from the Capote clan since Mom died.

Before I could offer *extensive* insight into the misguidedness of Octo's crush, he managed to steer the conversation back onto me. "Actually, it's really Sherman who's the lovelorn one. He's got it bad for an Icon."

"A *deity*?" Hank gasped. "Well, check *you* right out, Sherman Capote!"

"How *progressive*." Urta looked impressed. "You kids today."

"Have you asked her on a date yet?" asked Hank.

Octo tentacle-slapped me on the back and let out a raucous, cephalopod guffaw. Hank and Urta pressed their beaks against the glass, awaiting more gory details.

"I'm planning to ask her to the Prom," I said. "But it's not for four weeks. I have time."

Hank pointed a tentacle straight at me. "Has your brain dried out? An Icon expects—"

"Sherman," Urta gasped. "You have *no* time!"

Hank intertwined his tentacles with Urta's. "When I first saw this fine specimen of sea life, do you think I waited one minute to ask her to the Enchantment Under the Sea dance?"

"Um," I said, looking to Octo who shook his head like he'd heard this one a thousand times. "I'm guessing . . . no?"

"Exactly," said Hank. "I swept her off her tentacles!"

Octo put down his sea moss. "You know what, buddy? It's true. What if you finally ask Juliet to the Prom, and she says no? What if someone else asks her first? You need to lay groundwork now, buckaroo."

"But you said—"

I wasn't sure if it was okay to mention the races in front of Octo's folks, so I stopped talking. I just sat there, chewing on the surprisingly delicious alien seaweed. I thought the whole point of the let's-win-the-Rocket-Races project was that it'd make actually *asking* Juliet . . . well, kind of a formality.

Because I'd be cool then, right?

On the other hand, risking a "no" from Juliet meant a crushed planet, not just a crushed Capote.

Maybe these ventitents were right. I had to man up.

"There's a double bill at the drive-in on Saturday," Octo said.

"Show her that you're interested," Hank agreed. "You must woo her before asking such a big commitment of her."

"Think of it as a prelude to the Prom," said Octo. "A warm-up date."

"Maybe even make it a double date," added Hank. "Eh, son?"

"Let's just focus on Sherman's love life," Octo said.

"But I don't even have a car," I said. "I can't walk to the drive-in."

Octo piped up. "Hey Hank, Sherman can use the Toyota for the drive-in, right?"

"If it's for love," his dad said, "certainly."

"Okay, I'll ask her," I said.

How hard could it be?

CHAPTER TWENTY-TWO

The War of the Worlds

Later that week, I loitered outside the auditorium, nervously waiting for Juliet to emerge. The hallway was packed with students shuffling between classes, but I was in my own little world. I spotted a scrunched-up candy wrapper made of transparent cellophane. Each time the doors swooshed open it sailed on the breeze, then got sucked back when they swooshed closed. I could see faint AJABot caterpillar-tracks on the linoleum floor, a collection of dust bunnies that might have been mating like, well, bunnies, and a spider scurrying up its web between the wall socket and the doorstop. It's amazing what you notice when the last thing you want to think about is what you're about to do.

Trying to do.

I was so distracted that I was even accidentally nice to Jess.

"Excellent acting today," I said as she swanned by with three note-taking Martians in tow.

"Talk not to me, for I'll not speak a word," she declared, "do as thou wilt, for I am done with thee." Then she punched me on the arm, stuck out her tongue and joined the mass of alien life forms bustling down the corridor. She was still annoyed that she had been cast in the supporting role of Lady Capulet and not the lead.

As I waited for my Juliet to appear, something tugged at my sleeve. A some*one*.

"Sherman Capote!" squealed a little Martian, with a wide, toothless grin. He gazed up at me with his giant shiny black eyes. He'd just eaten a tangerine, or maybe Martians naturally smell of tangerines.

"Um, hi . . . "

"Klaatu!" he said in his cyber-chipmunk voice. "You remember Klaatu?"

"Oh, hey, Klaatu," I said, shuffling my feet. "I'm kind of in the middle of something here."

"Yes," he agreed. "Standing in the corner, staring into space."

"It's called waiting," I explained.

He pulled a flyer from his little backpack and pressed it into my hands. "Stimulation while you wait!

Vital instructional information for the Prom! All must prepare!"

The flyer showed a gigantic mechanical tripod war machine about to smash through London Bridge. It was an old-fashioned, pen-and-ink-style drawing. And above it, written like a vintage newspaper headline, one word:

PROM!

"That's great, thanks, Klaatu," I said, just as his jumpsuit started to twinkle, reflecting something iridescently, astonishingly, heartbreakingly blue.

"Hello, Sherman."

My wait was over. I looked up, saw Juliet's luminous, perfect face peering around the auditorium door and instinctively stuffed the flyer into the back pocket of my jeans.

"Hey, Juliet, I'm ... er ... " I stuttered. "What a coincidence to bump into you here."

"He was waiting," stated Klaatu.

"Well . . . I was wondering if, well . . . would you mind if I asked you about something? If you're not busy?"

Pull yourself together, Capote.

"I was hoping to speak with you, too," Juliet said.

The idea she'd thought about me, even for a moment,

caused a burst of happy electricity to tickle me all over, including, strangely, my left butt cheek.

That was actually Klaatu pulling the flyer out of my jeans pocket.

"Store . . . keep . . . yes," he said, "but also read! Read the instructional information, Sherman Capote! All must prepare!"

Even though at this particular moment this particular Martian was driving me nuts, there was something incredibly comforting about the little guys. They reminded me of the two pre-schoolers who lived across the street from us in Geilenkirchen, always waiting for me to come home from school to show off their paintings and ask for piggybacks.

And yet Octo had hyped the Martians as ace racers. It was a weird contrast.

"Really?" I said to Juliet, trying my best to ignore the Martian. "You were hoping to speak with me?"

"I was," she said, floating into the corridor. "I wanted to apologize."

I realized that no one walking past in the corridor could take their eyes off her. Meanwhile Klaatu had flattened out the creased flyer and was holding it up to me.

"Sherman Capote!" he chirped.

"Apologize?" I said to Juliet. "For what?"

"I gave you so little to work with in the orchard scene today," Juliet said. "I was . . . distracted."

"Are you crazy?" I said. "You were great."

Klaatu proudly produced another flyer from his backpack.

"Thank you, Klaatu, you're too kind," Juliet said.

The little Martian's head bobbled from right to left. "She knows Klaatu's name!" he giggled.

Juliet smiled and rubbed his bulbous, gray head affectionately.

Lucky little Martian.

Octo was right. I had it bad.

"Look! Read!" Klaatu called to us both. "The theme for the Prom is *The War of the Worlds!*"

I'd thought that maybe I should just ask her to Prom, right then and there. But Octo's plan played in my spinning brain. *Date first, then Prom.*

"I love that movie," I said, bracing myself. "Speaking of movies—"

"*The War of the Worlds,* the *book!*" Klaatu corrected. "Written in 1898, by the Englishman of this planet known as Herbert George Wells!"

"Oh, the ethnocentric guy?" I said, thinking of Jessica's essay.

"That sounds out of this world," said Juliet with a smile.

"No, in this world," corrected Klaatu.

"What I was hoping," I said, trying to blurt it out, "was if you'd maybe like to—"

But Klaatu grabbed my left arm with both his little hands.

"Not the other adaptations," he said. "Not the Orson Welles radio broadcast of 1938—"

"If maybe I'd like to what?" Juliet asked, tipping her head slightly to one side and giving me a smile that could have powered Nevada for the next millennium.

" . . . nor the George Pal motion picture of 1953—"

"If . . . um . . . " I stuttered.

" . . . nor the presently touring arena show, or the Steven Spielberg motion picture of 2005 . . . "

Motion picture.

I took a deep breath and went for it. "If you'd maybe-want-to-like-to-if-you're-not-too-busy-go-to-a-movie-with-me on-Saturday."

Juliet blinked. It was the longest moment of my life. I felt as small as a Martian as I waited for whatever hair-washing or party-hopping excuse she'd dump on me.

I knew who I was going to blame for this whole date-first-Prom-later idea. And I vowed, in future, to ignore any and all advice they dished out over deep-fried seaweed.

Juliet looked down, almost distracted. "I've never noticed that spider web before."

"I've even got wheels for the night," I added. "So maybe you could just, I dunno, beam in at eight, at the drive-in?"

Beam in at eight. Nice line, Señor Suave. But I didn't want to admit that I wasn't actually allowed to drive Hank's Toyota. I was only allowed to sit in it while parked.

The corridor crowd thinned out and even Klaatu, to my overwhelming relief, finally finished his verbal briefing of every *War of the Worlds* adaptation and vamoosed to his next class, just like Juliet and I were supposed to do. She leaned against the auditorium doors, her semi-transparent arms folded, and raised her unbelievable crystal eyes back to me.

"A movie? A fabricated reality projected onto a screen designed to distract humans while they eat exploded kernels of corn?"

"Exactly! Popcorn."

"Do you know," she said, as if I ought to, "I've actually never *seen* a movie before. What distractions will be displayed?"

"Unmissable classics," I said. "*Independence Day* and *Mars Attacks.*"

"And should I bring ears of corn to explode?" she asked.

"No, no, that's . . . fine," I said. "I'll get the popcorn, but is that a 'yes'?"

Even as I asked, I heard tiny footsteps scurrying along the now-deserted corridor, and Klaatu's sci-fi cartoon voice getting louder and louder – "No no no no no no no!" – until he pretty much crashed into my legs.

"Not *Independence Day*!" he said. "Not *Mars Attacks*! Nothing in any way *inspired* by *The War of the Worlds* either! Only *The War of the Worlds*, the *book*, Sherman Capote!"

"1898," Juliet said to Klaatu.

"By Herbert George Wells," I said.

"Yes," Juliet said, looking back at me. "That's a yes."

CHAPTER TWENTY-THREE

Stranded at the Drive-In

I basked in the glory of Juliet's *yes*, but I still had to get through the week. I distracted myself from the excitement and nerves of my first ever date by means of a full schedule of daytime classes and nocturnal rocket building. The ship was really coming together, and despite feeling sleepy during the day, I was even keeping up with the alien subjects.

Well, most of them.

My academic black mark was Galactic Languages, GalLang. I had no ear for Earthly foreign languages, let alone alien lingos, but our teacher, Mrs Rackles, sure did. She looked like a giant, green ear – a large audio receptor on four legs.

She was patient with me as I butchered verb conjugation in dozens of alien languages, only once muttering, "It's only Earthlings that expect all aliens to speak their languages."

Sonya was a star pupil in GalLang. Maybe it was from her years of Balleropera training, or maybe it was natural talent, but she picked up the galactic slang like a local, effortlessly reciting poems in foreign tongues while the rest of us struggled to say, "We come in peace."

I did, however, finally find my footing on the football field. Octo was a sharp shooter when it came to throwing the pigskin and Atawee had clearly put the word out that I was not to be maimed, so I caught the ball with panache and made spectacular touchdowns.

Did I mind that my on-field prowess was only due to an alien protection racket? Nah. It felt great. For once, Sherman Capote was the guy that everyone wanted on their team.

Dad even stopped by between meetings one day to watch part of a game. I was pretty sure it wasn't a figment of my imagination when I saw him nodding from the stands when the final whistle blew. He wasn't clapping, but he wasn't shaking his head in frustration either.

It was progress.

So by Saturday night, date night with Juliet, I was actually feeling pretty confident. Like me, the drive-in pulsed with anticipation.

It was a Groom Lake tradition, and almost everyone from school was there. But unlike the cafeteria, with its strict social hierarchy, this parking lot with a view was a free-for-all. Rows upon rows of personal space cruisers, winged jet packs, and the occasional military Jeep faced a large white screen propped up by two adult-sized AJABots.

Octo had parked Hank's Toyota for me smack dab in the center. I waited anxiously for Juliet to materialize beside me and watched the Groom Lake kids let loose.

A couple of Xenophine Reeds were playing Frisbee, a gaggle of Martians arranged lawn chairs on top of their low-rider saucer, and the AJABot kids danced to the beat of their own techno. Atawee was there, holding claws with his scorpion companion in what looked like a missile on wheels, if Ferrari made missiles.

It was definitely date night in Groom Lake. The sweet scent of frying onions and roasting hot dogs from the concession stand at the back wafted over the coupled teenagers, hoping to make out in parked spaceships.

I even spotted Sonya's Eggcraft, a few rows in front. She sat cross-legged on the roof with Houston, and I wondered if they were on a date, or just here as friends. I thought about going over to say hello, but they looked like they were having a good time, laughing and talking, and didn't need any Sherman interruption. Besides, I had to stay on target.

The truck's clock read 19:58. My heart started to pound and my palms got sweaty.

I tried to sink out of view as Jessica and her Prom committee crew strolled by, munching on hot dogs and chewing on gossip.

"Look at my poor loser brother," she said, and then she sang a song I recognized from mornings waiting for her to stop using the shower as her private rehearsal space:

"Stranded at the drive-in, branded a fool . . ."

"She's materializing at eight, okay?" I said. "Now Grease Lightning outta here."

"What will they say Monday at school?"

"You have ketchup on your cheek," I lied. But she swiped at her face anyway.

The whole gang mooched off, chuckling at my comedienne sister, still singing. I would've drowned her out with some Foo Fighters from the radio if it hadn't been for the glow that suddenly flickered over the dashboard.

I checked the clock.

20:00.

Exactly on time.

I hadn't seen Juliet materialize since she was late for Drama that first day – this time I was much, much closer to the action.

Her spherical blue cloud, so bright I had to squint, zapped into existence right above the passenger seat. The hairs on my arms and the back of my neck stood on end. The cloud grew arms, then legs, and then the little cardboard air-freshener tree hanging from the rearview mirror started spinning like crazy – until, finally, Juliet was right next to me, floating an inch or so above the seat, looking perplexed by what she saw on the screen.

"I didn't think movies would be this . . . interpretative," she said quietly.

I followed her confused gaze to the white screen.

"Oh, it hasn't started yet," I explained. "Don't worry, we're not here to watch a white rabbit running in the snow."

"Though that does sound lovely," she said with a smile.

"I can't believe you've never seen a movie before," I said.

"My parents are very . . . traditional," she said. "But I want to experience everything that the universe has to offer."

"Well, I'm glad your first time will be with me," I blurted. "I can still remember my first movie."

"Was it the white rabbit one?"

Gorgeous, and a sense of humor. *What's not to love?*

"I was six," I said, "and we were on a base in South Korea. The Air Force got a print of the original *Star Wars*, not the so-called Special Edition ones with all that phony CGI, and not the silly prequels, but the classic – the best."

I was rambling, but powerless to stop myself. *Star Wars* had that effect on me. Or perhaps it was Juliet.

"The four of us – my family – went to this art deco cinema, and it was packed. All of the adults had seen the film before, of course, but they wanted to take their kids to see it on the big screen. I don't think I blinked for two hours. It's probably what got me interested in space, and building rockets, and . . . "

I was totally geeking out, drooling over Millennium Falcons, in front of an alien who spends every day in thousands of worlds. "Sorry," I said, "that probably sounds silly to you."

"Not at all," she said. "It's sweet. I didn't get to do those kinds of things with my parents. They were always away on Icon business. I was pretty much raised by my

Mentors. My parents seem to be more interested in the universe than they are in their own daughter."

We had more in common than I'd thought.

"My mom and dad were away a lot too, but usually not at the same time. And now, it's just my dad."

"Is it your mother's turn to be away?"

I didn't want our date to be a downer before it had even begun, but I didn't want to lie.

"My mom was a nurse in the army and she was training a whole new hospital of nurses in Afghanistan, and, well . . . she's not coming back, ever."

"I'm sorry, Sherman. I sometimes take for granted that we're immortal."

"So you'll never lose your parents?"

"No. But they're gone so much I sort of feel like I already have."

The air was heavy and I needed to change the subject. Luckily, the drive-in lights dimmed and a sign projected onscreen telling us to tune our radios to AM 590.

I fiddled with the Toyota's digital tuner until the cab filled with static.

"Are you excited?" I asked.

"I love it actually," she said, as the 20th Century Fox drumroll escalated into the familiar fanfare. "I've never seen a monument to giant numbers before."

"And it gets better," I said as the film began.

Juliet was immediately transfixed by the sound and images, staring at the screen like a glowing blue statue. But I couldn't shake the feeling that once the lights came up she'd just say, "Thank you and goodnight," and that'd be it. I needed to impress her, roll this date into *the big one*. Prom.

So by the time Jeff Goldblum realized the aliens' signal was a countdown, I was feeling a little panicked, worrying about the future here on Earth, not about the aliens onscreen.

I nearly jumped out of my seat when Octo tapped at my open window.

"How's your mojo, Romeo?" he whispered.

Juliet, luckily, was entranced in movieland. I double-checked, then consulted the cephalopod.

"I dunno, she's kind of in her own little world over there."

"Will Smith has that effect on the ladies," Octo explained. "It's universal."

"You think I should put my arm around her?" I whispered back.

Octo pulled an are-all-Earth-kids-this-dumb face, then ticked off a list with his tentacles.

"Popcorn first, then tentacle . . . I mean *arm* – sorry

– then snuggle, and then maybe smooch," he said. "Are you new to this or something?"

I was. I was a complete rookie, and way out of my league.

Popcorn.

The one thing Juliet had asked about!

I'd people-watched, I'd yelled at Jess, I'd even stared at the stars, but I'd completely forgotten to buy popcorn.

"Dude," Octo said, noting its absence in the truck's cab. "Seriously, you need to score the corn. It's how your tentacles touch for the first time."

"Fingers," I corrected him.

"Nah, they give me indigestion," he said. "Anyway, the way it works is, you watch the movie, you both go for a scoop of the salty stuff and then you make first contact. You both pretend it was just an accident, and you have a little stand-off: are you or aren't you going to pull away? But it's just a game because you both knew where scooping salted kernels would lead. You do cute little embarrassed giggles, and you catch each other's eyes, telling each other, 'Hey, it's okay, I'm in this tub of buttered corn with you, baby, we're in it together,' and then, and only *then*, is there snuggle potential."

"Wow," I said. "How do you know all of this?"

"Ancient wisdom, dude," he said. "Only once you

173

get an arm around her can you go for the smooch. Otherwise she'll see you coming a mile away. You've gotta *flank* in from the snuggle."

"Could you get us the popcorn?" I pleaded.

"For someone in the same species as Darwin, you don't know much about natural selection, do you?"

I shook my head as Goldblum tried to convince the skeptical, and surprisingly youthful, President to evacuate the White House.

"You getting the popcorn proves to Juliet that you can provide for her. It's simple hunter-gatherer stuff. She's in the cave, and you're out hunting the woolly mammoth! It's natural selection, dude. And you want Juliet to select you! Dontcha?"

"Naturally," I said. He was right. I had to hunt the mammoth, bring its hide back to the cave. "I'll get the corn."

"Be quick," Octo whispered. "And just remember the code: P.A.S.S."

"Popcorn, Arm, Snuggle, Smooch," I said.

Octo slinked off between cars with a gyroscopic tentacle-shimmy and I leaned in towards my Icon date.

"Juliet, I'm just going to pop out to get the popcorn."

"Go!" she shouted, without taking her eyes off the

scrambling White House staff. I wasn't sure if she was talking to me or to the President's soon-to-be-incinerated lackeys. Either way, I was going hunting for my cave-girl.

But as I double-timed it towards the concession, someone else moved in on my cave. I turned back to check on Juliet as I ran and spotted NED casually leaning against her window, clicking his long, ultra-white fingers to get her attention. My first instinct was to return to the car and defend my cave. But if I returned empty-handed, it would show Juliet that I couldn't provide.

I blame you, Charles Darwin!

I rocked up to the concession stand to find Lunch Lady Nancy moonlighting behind the snack bar. "We're closed, sweetheart," she drawled.

"Wait, what?" I yelped. "We're not even halfway through the first movie!"

"Union rules."

"Please, Nancy," I said, "just one box of popcorn. It's to save the planet."

"I'd love to help, but I don't get overtime and you don't get popcorn."

She pulled down the rolling metal barrier over the window, and over my mission.

On the screen, a bunch of crazy-types were waving

signs on the roof of a skyscraper. One of them read "Please Take Me Away From Here".

That's exactly how I felt. But unlike those sign-waving idiots, I knew exactly what would happen if I didn't fix this debacle: the end of the world.

Somehow – even though I was about to trudge back to the truck without the mammoth – I had to win this girl's heart. Wimping out just wasn't an option.

"Hey, cumin bean, you want some corn?" It was one of the Fungi kids, a football-sized mushroom, peeping out from behind the concession stand. His smirky little black eyes narrowed at me. "Pretty hard to come by after eight-thirty."

"Do you have some?" I asked, desperately.

"I might," the Fungus replied. "Do you have fifteen bucks?"

Slowly, in his wormy little fingers, the mushroom pulled out a box from behind his back. The red-and-white striped carton was overflowing with popcorn that spilled to the concrete every time he moved.

"I might," I replied, checking my Space Shuttle Columbia wallet. "Ten. That's all I've got. It's a good deal."

"Sixty," the Fungus countered.

"What?"

"Three."

"Have you ever haggled before?" I asked.

"Zip it, primate," he said. "Forty-two. Final offer."

I held out my lone, crumpled ten-dollar bill and said, "How about a portable portrait of Alexander Hamilton? Founding father and America's first secretary of the treasury."

He snatched the note off me.

"Sucker," he cackled, handing me the box. The not-so-fun guy bounced over the wire fence, disappearing into the night.

I was ten dollars poorer, but I'd bagged the mammoth. I was back in the evolutionary game.

Buoyed by my negotiating skills, I turned back towards the Toyota to politely but firmly tell NED to leave us alone so Juliet and I could watch the world's landmarks get blown to pieces. In peace.

But something was definitely, unmistakably, *off*.

It'd unnerved me, ever since NED showed up, that his furry-faced bodyguard wasn't in sight. That was new. And I couldn't help feeling that this whole black-market-popcorn thing had the distinct atmosphere of a . . .

"HELLO, TINY, DEFENSELESS—"

. . . set-up.

"—HUMAN."

Graz rose from behind the industrial-sized garbage container next to the snack stand. He towered above me – gray-black fur stinking of wet dog and hot dog, piercing orange cat's eyes staring down at me, razor-teeth fighting for room in his mouth – and it all pretty much fell into place.

Never trust a fungus selling snacks.

Whether NED, Graz and the mushroom had planned the whole thing in advance, or if it was more spontaneous, I didn't know. But by the time I was upside down, seven feet above the ground, showering piles of half-eaten wieners and ketchup-soaked bun fragments with my stash of fresh, delicious popcorn, the mechanics of the set-up didn't really matter. I wondered if this was how Alexander Hamilton felt when facing Aaron Burr. Totally. Utterly. Ambushed.

The fuzz-monster growled, "GRAZ NEVER LEAVES A JOB HALF-DONE, *SHER*-MAN."

Just as the onscreen, make-believe aliens zapped the White House and the whole drive-in vibrated with the explosion, real-live alien Graz buried me deep in the container. My head *clanged* against the bottom and I blacked out.

★　★　★

I woke to someone hurling giant eels at me.

It turned out to be Octo slapping my cheeks with his slippery tentacles. He must have pulled me from the garbage and leaned me against the bin and now – for the second time in a month – he was checking my bones for fractures.

"What happened to you?"

I gazed at the stars, inhaled the romantic aroma of dusty concrete and rotting sausage, and explained my encounter.

"For never was a story of more woe," I concluded. "Than this of Juliet and her *Sherm-eo*."

"But are you *okay*, dude?" Octo said. "Took forever to find you. How many tentacles?"

"What?"

"How many tentacles am I holding up?"

"Seven," I mumbled.

"You're fine, Romeo," the ventitent declared.

But I wasn't. I had to get back to my date.

I pulled a ketchup-smeared popcorn carton off my head and scrounged for useable kernels. "I've got to get back to the Toyota and bring Juliet her mammoth."

"Err . . . hmm . . . " Octo stuttered, "well . . . y'see . . . it's not-too-spectacular news there, buckaroo."

Then I heard it over the speakers, the opening scene

of *Mars Attacks* that meant that *Independence Day* was over. I'd been blacked out for well over an hour. "Don't tell me," I groaned. "Juliet thinks I abandoned her."

"It's a bit worse than that," Octo warned. "It seems she, ah, didn't want to stay for Tim Burton's underrated masterpiece, so she—"

"She dematerialized?" I sighed. "I'm such a moron. If *only* I'd remembered to buy the stupid—"

"No, Sherm," Octo said. "She left with NED."

CHAPTER TWENTY-FOUR

Test Drive

After that star-crossed night, Juliet completely avoided me outside of rehearsal. She materialized just in time for our scenes, stayed in character while on stage, but then *poof* – she'd zap somewhere else as soon as rehearsal finished. Since I'd messed up our first, and possibly only, date, all of my hopes were riding on *The Plan*.

It was a long shot, but my only shot.

Could Sonya, Houston, Octo and I could build a champion rocket racer? Could I fly the thing well enough to blow away the competition? Would Juliet then realize I was the only man in the universe for her – that I was Prom material?

These were big questions bashing around in my brain, and they gave me a headache. So I did exactly what Dad does when he's upset: I threw myself into my work.

Every night, our racer inched closer to resembling Houston's 3D model. It was evolving into a thing of physical beauty. This rocket was actually *two* rockets with a cockpit and cabin resting on top, a bit like a skier wearing a backpack. Of course, these skis were fusion-powered and could propel the skier at more than a thousand miles per hour, but you get the idea.

"It's a double-clutch fusion system," Houston announced, "something an Earthbound rocketeer such as yourself would normally find rather unfamiliar. But I've developed an interface that's similar to an Earth-type motor vehicle."

"You mean it'll be like driving a car?" I asked.

"Like a really fast, flying car," said Octo.

"But I don't even have a license," I confessed.

"Don't worry so much, Sherman," said Sonya. "You picked up Eggcraft flying pretty quickly, I'm sure you'll be ace at this. And we've built in plenty of practice time."

"Thanks, guys," I said. "It means a lot that you have so much faith in me."

It was great to be part of something, part of a team with a big, lofty goal. But all of this nocturnal construction was starting to take its toll. I was sleepwalking through school. Before long, Dad got a note from Principal

Meltzer about my nodding off in lessons and asked if I had glandular fever.

Jessica valiantly sprang to my defense. "There's no way anybody would ever kiss Sherman."

At least my friends had faith in me.

★　★　★

It was late Saturday afternoon, the one weekiversary of my date debacle, and I was waiting for Octo to pick me up. I wasn't feeling very upbeat – I was starting to think that Juliet was a lost cause. As soon as I jumped into the truck, I began complaining that maybe she just wasn't into me.

"Do *not* despair!" said Octo, as we approached the hangar. "Romeo didn't give up on *his* Juliet."

"Octo, Romeo and Juliet die at the end," I said.

"What?!" he shouted, his twenty tentacles flailing all over. "Coulda used a spoiler alert there!"

"Are you guys ready?" asked Sonya, who was loitering with Houston outside the closed hangar doors. She was wearing blue overalls covered in logos and patches saying *Race Ace Fusion Oil*, *Beeble's Booster Emporium* and *Snap-On Tools*. Houston was sporting a toolbelt that looked like a lightsaber collection. They were both so covered in oil and grime they looked positively alien. Houston passed me a bottle of cream soda.

"Thanks," I said. "I'm parched."

"It's not for you," said Sonya. "It's for *her.*"

I looked around, secretly hoping that Juliet had come to visit. But she hadn't. "Who?"

Octo slid open the rattling, corrugated-iron doors, then disappeared into the dark hangar.

"That's for you to decide," said Sonya. "We came early today and finished the paint job. She's ready to race in the trials tomorrow."

"But you get the naming privileges," said Houston, as the hangar lights popped on.

I stood with my three best friends – the ventitent, the robot, and the lizard – and marveled at our feat of astrophysics engineering. The twin rockets were silver-sleek, with a double racing stripe, green and black, running down the double fuselage, and four stabilizing fins at the rear. The front cockpit and rear cabin, perched atop the rockets, looked like the nose of an F-18 fused with a postal van.

"Isn't she *magnificent?*" Sonya asked.

Octo folded a few tentacles and gave me a proud-as-punch, three-beaked grin.

"So," he said, "whadaya gonna name her?"

There was never any question.

"Carol," I said, smashing the cream soda bottle. "I think Mom would like having a rocket named after her."

"Then let's take Carol for a test drive," said Sonya. "Fire her up and she'll purr like a canary."

"Kitten," I corrected her.

"Oh, no, thanks," she said. "I've already eaten."

Houston wheeled out the steel box containing the Aldrin suit. "You must get used to the ecto-shell," he explained.

When I stepped into the suit, it gripped me. It squeezed every muscle in my body, fusing with my form. At first I thought I'd feel claustrophobic, but the ecto-suit became part of me. It was seamless.

"How's your vision?" Houston asked.

His voice echoed in my head loud and clear. The other voices less so, like Sonya and Octo were just standing nearby, using Houston as a microphone.

"Great," I replied. The vision was digitally enhanced and I could see everything in super-sharp detail. "It's like mega-HD."

Octo wheeled the rocket to the edge of the desert and helped me up and into the cockpit. I settled into a replica of my dad's Jeep.

"It should feel familiar," he said.

"Grab the wheel," Sonya said, "and Carol will respond."

The instant I did, a mass of read-outs flashed into existence in the air in front of me. I gradually recognized all the virtual dials for speed, pitch, yaw . . . everything. The controls stayed in perfect focus wherever I turned my head.

"This is *awesome*."

"Pay attention," Houston said. "I know you understand the basics from your Eggcraft experience, but it's vital you familiarize yourself with this particular class of low-altitude competitive rocket. We shall proceed step-by-step. Understood?"

"Understood," I said, in no hurry to vaporize myself first time round.

The racer's fusion system throbbed beneath me – a deep, teeth-rattling hum. And maybe it was static electricity in the suit or something, but I was convinced my hair was trying to stand on end.

"This thing *is* safe, right?" I asked.

"Pretty safe," Sonya said, not entirely filling me with confidence.

"Only one way to find out, right?" Octo said.

"We're going for a ten-mile, four-hundred-miles-per-hour burst," Houston said. "Your only goal is to keep a straight line."

"Got it," I said. "Straight line. Ten miles. Four-hundred-miles-per-hour."

"Depress clutch, Sherman," Houston instructed. "That's the one on the left."

I pressed down with my left foot. "Clutch is depressed."

"Maybe we should cheer it up," chuckled Octo.

"Hush your beaks," snapped Sonya. "This is serious."

"Apply accelerator . . . " said Houston.

I pressed down the second farthest right of the pedals.

" . . . *very* gently."

And the racer bolted.

The fusion system, which sounded like twenty giants yelling "AHHHHHHH!" at the same time, propelled me into the vast Nevada desert. The G-force must have been incredible, but the suit protected me from feeling it.

"I said *gently*!" Houston yelled, his voice reverberating in my helmet.

The salt flats became a blurry white ocean beneath me. It was only when a stray boulder or tumbleweed *whizzed* by that I got any sense of just how brain-meltingly fast I was actually going.

Even the dazzling, red-orange Nevada sunset seemed

to be getting closer.

Awesome.

"Try a turn, buckaroo!" Octo urged.

"Do not attempt a turn, Sherman," Houston said. "Keep her straight and steady."

"You crash that thing and you're *toast*, Earthman," Sonya yelled.

"Who brought toast?" asked Octo.

"I'm gonna try a turn, Houston," I said. "Trust me."

"Sonya, could you order pizza?" Octo continued.

"Sherman, no," said Houston, "the suit—"

I turned the wheel. Just a *touch* . . .

The horizon tilted. And kept tilting. Until it had spun right around, and then kept tilting, kept rotating.

"Sherman," Houston said calmly, "you're in a death-spiral."

"I'm going to die?" I shouted.

"Don't worry!" Octo yelled. "I'm filming this on my phone. It's spectacular!"

"SMALL MOVEMENTS, SHERMAN," Sonya hollered.

"The suit enhances your strength," Houston said. "You need to be gentle and precise. You also need to DO AS YOU'RE TOLD."

"Okay, okay," I said. "But what *now*?"

"Idiot!" Sonya yelled.

"Beautiful!" Octo yelled. "This is great footage!"

The sky was spinning so fast now it was making me think of Jessica's kaleidoscope. The one I broke when I was eight. Jessica took her revenge by filling my lunch box with Goose's dog food.

"Holy cow," I said, "I think my life's flashing before me."

But the flashes didn't last long. I still had so much I wanted to do. I had a deity to take to Prom and a planet to save. Plus, I really wanted to be old enough to walk into R-rated movies without sneaking in the back door. I had a lot of living to do; I didn't want to die in a fiery ball of wreckage. So I decided to focus.

"I'm putting you on automatic pilot and activating the homing beacon," Houston said.

"Wait," I pleaded. "Just give me a second. I can do this!"

Gentle.

I just needed be gentle and precise.

I eased my breathing, let the info from the instruments flow into my brain like I was conjuring The Force. I held the steering column dead still and gradually got my bearings. The racer reacted to my moves and the spin gradually slowed until chaos gave way to control.

I could see the desert again, now in crisp, clear focus instead of a nauseating blur. And with the racer back under my command, I cruised straight and smooth. And safe.

"That's good piloting, Sherman," Houston said. "Carol's homing beacon is activated. Just bring her home."

The homing beacon was both a *blip* I could hear and a glowing dot superimposed on my vision. But before I followed the glowing breadcrumbs back, I wanted to master this low-orbit rocketeering.

I pushed into a controlled turn, lifting the rocket up and back on itself in an aerial loop. I'd watched enough air shows on enough air bases to know the tricks and manoeuvres that pilots use to show they're top gun. I did banks, nosedives and twists, all narrated by Houston's protests. But I was pretty sure that Carol loved it.

I pushed the racer to its limits. Swoops. Turns. Glides.

And then I finally felt it.

Six degrees of freedom.

6DoF.

Over the years I'd built dozens of rockets. And I'd watched each one soar into the sky while I'd stayed on *terra firma.* But now that I was airborne, I felt at home up here in the night sky. Maybe Octo was right, maybe all this time the thing holding me back had been . . . me.

It was time to let myself go. It was time to reach for the stars.

CHAPTER TWENTY-FIVE

The Balcony Scene

I parked the rocket in the hangar and climbed out feeling like an experienced pilot. The suit peeled off me with a *zzzzzzCLINK* as it loosened its grip. I kept my eyes closed as ordered, and suddenly, instead of the tangy, metallic smell of ecto-suit, I could smell cinnamon-scented desert air, hot Grav-Thwart plating, cooling fusion engines and . . . pepperoni.

"Did you guys order pizza?" I asked.

"Don't sweat it," Sonya's voice said, "there's plenty left."

"Not for long," Octo mumbled with his beak full.

"*Now* open your eyes," Houston said, "but do not be alarmed. Your natural vision will need to readjust."

He was right.

For a moment I couldn't see anything but a smudgy grayness. My heart pounded and I felt rising panic, but then, gradually, shapes emerged through the fog.

The hangar's criss-cross superstructure and corrugated walls.

The racer's open cockpit and still-glowing dual exhausts.

The junk in the scrapyard.

And to be honest, I'd expected to see Octo, Sonya and Houston huddled around me. Applauding, maybe. Patting me on the back. But instead, Houston was carefully packing the Aldrin-suit into its container and Sonya was hurling pizzas Frisbee-style at Octo, who was catching them like an outfielder on the other side of the hangar, catching and chomping each one with his middle beak.

The pile of pizza boxes next to Sonya was as tall as her.

"The *What Beats a Pizza?* guy has a crush on me," she explained. "I'm on a 'buy one, get twenty free' plan, which is handy since Octo pretty much needs one pizza per tentacle. Want one?"

"No thanks," I said. All that looping had left my stomach in knots. Exhilarated, adrenaline-fueled knots, but knots all the same. "I've got something I need to do."

"Are you *kidding*?" Octo yelled, his super-bass voice echoing around the place. "It's *pizza!*"

In truth, my stomach wasn't just in knots from the aerobatics. Plus, I had to put things right with Juliet.

"As far as Juliet's concerned," I explained, "I stranded her at the drive-in. If I've got any chance of pulling off Mission *Prom*possible, I've got to explain what happened. Romeo didn't give up and neither will I."

"Um, dude, Romeo dies at the end."

"Spoiler alert, Octo," I said with a salute.

I opened the hangar door and raced through the quiet Area 51 evening. Being Saturday, the drive-in was open, and I knew it was showing *The Day the Earth Stood Still*, the original. As I panted my way through the empty suburban streets, it did actually feel like the Earth was standing still. At the same time, I knew the world was spinning, the days were passing and the NEDs were on their way.

I searched the base, looking for Juliet's unmistakable blue glow. I found it emanating from a blue ship parked beside the Slurp-n-Go convenience store. The smooth, rounded-pyramid-shaped starship was glowing above a vacant plot. Everything about it felt regal, like a rocket-propelled palace.

So once I'd climbed the steps on the nearest leg and was about to press the surprisingly doorbell-like button next to the hatchway, I couldn't help feeling like a trespasser who was about to get arrested.

Or worse.

But I pressed it anyway – just as a bunch of chattering Martians (probably offended by the portrayal of aliens in *The Day the Earth Stood Still*) left the Slurp-n-Go carrying slushy SLURPMEs and chips – and I rehearsed my line in my head.

Hey, Juliet, I'm really sorry about the drive-in.

Silently, the hatchway slid open. In the darkness I saw a hand reach for a switch just inside the door.

Hey, Juliet, I'm sorry that I got stuffed into the garbage container.

Strangely, it was a human hand.

A woman's hand.

My stomach tightened. My pulse pounded. But I had no idea why – until the switch *blipped* softly and light flooded the doorway and the hand's owner looked me right in the eye. It felt just like the moment Jessica and I first walked into the cafeteria that first morning.

My brain went into a high-pitched ALERT; like an interior air-raid siren, yelling at my eyes and telling them that there was no way what they were seeing could be real.

It was my mother.

"Are you just going to stand there, trespassing? Or are you going to come inside?"

And then I fainted.

CHAPTER TWENTY-SIX

Mentor Interruptus

I woke up in my old bedroom. In Geilenkirchen, Germany. The one with the cracked window and the swirly carpet that smelled of candles. Juliet and my mother – my *mother*! – were leaning over me, looking concerned.

"I'm not sure the room is helping," Juliet whispered. "I think it's confusing him."

Mom felt my forehead. Checked my pulse.

"Agreed," she said. "Though this species confuses easily."

As Juliet helped me sit up, Geilenkirchen faded away and my bedroom became a room that was, well, white. Completely. Totally. White. No floor or walls or ceiling. The bed transformed into a hovering slab of cold metal.

"Mom . . . ?" I murmured. "Is that really . . . "

I felt tears coming the moment I spoke. With one hand I hid my eyes from Juliet.

"I am not anyone's mother," Mom began, in her stern, do-your-homework-young-man voice.

"I don't understand. What do you mean? I'm really confused."

"You *see*?" she said to Juliet.

"This is my Mentor," explained Juliet. "She's wearing a borrowed look. She came to Earth without telling me—"

"Because her parents were getting concerned about how much time she was spending on this primitive planet," Mom cut in.

"Even though I call twice a day," chimed Juliet, "and leave messages that are never returned."

I was clearly caught in the middle of some intergalactic nanny tension, but I still had no idea how Juliet's minder was my mother.

"But, Mom?"

"I needed a physical form here," the Mentor-Mom began, "and when I beamed to your planet I came across a speck of human DNA in low orbit. To save time shopping for a look on the ground, I absorbed the DNA into my essence, adopting the look of the human known as Carol Capote. It's really not that hard to understand."

But it was. And my head hurt from trying. Or maybe it was from the fainting, or the facing an interstellar clone of my mom. Or maybe it was from the sheer disappointment of seeing her again – only for it not to be her. My brain felt crushed and my heart felt smashed.

"Now that I've explained my presence here," she said, "it's about time you explain what you were doing crawling up an Icon's spaceship without an official invitation, young human."

"Yes," Juliet asked, "what are you doing here, Sherman?"

"I came to apologize, for the other night at the drive-in."

Juliet tensed, and shot me a little head shake.

"What did you drive in *to*?" asked the Mentor.

"Oh, um, nothing," I fibbed.

"No, go on," she said. "I insist."

"Well, I took Juliet to the movies the other night and—"

"WHAT?" shouted Imposter-Mom.

"I beamed into Sherman's car," Juliet began. "So technically, as he didn't even have to pay for me, he didn't so much take me as—"

"A parked car? With a human boy?" the Mentor gasped. "Well, it's a good thing I got here when I did. I pray to *Icon* that you didn't attempt a snuggle!"

"We didn't even make it to popcorn," I said, then turned to Juliet to explain what had happened. "I didn't mean to leave you alone. I went for the popcorn and then NED turned up and I couldn't return to the cave—"

"Ah, the NEDs are a better class of company, my dear," the Mentor said, tapping Juliet on the head she'd buried in her blue hands. Imposter-Mom turned to me. "Juliet, as you call her, is only allowed to date other deities. I do hope you understand that your little drive-in excursion was a one-time blip in her otherwise perfect social record."

"Mentor, please don't," Juliet pleaded.

"You see, Sherman Capote, the universe has an order and it's my duty – no, my privilege – to uphold that order by keeping this adventurous Icon-in-training from making the type of social missteps that could unleash chaos across the galaxies."

"How would going to a drive-in unleash chaos?" I asked.

"Wars have been fought over the hands of deities," the Mentor said sharply. "And as quaint as your little planet may seem, it hardly contains stock worthy of marrying an Icon."

Marrying?

"Um, I was just trying to buy her popcorn."

"Hmmm." She glared at me. "I've been around for centuries and I know where popcorn leads. It starts with popcorn, then an arm around her. Then a snuggle, and then as inevitable as a dying star going super-nova, you would smooch."

Wow, maybe Octo did know what he was talking about.

"And that super-nova smooch would create a black hole of reason, sucking away all social etiquette, resulting in a ghastly Pairing between mortal and Icon that would upset the careful, eons-old balance of power among the various deities that rule the universe, setting off an endless conflict that would consume all planets and destroy all life. So don't you tell me that you had no idea where popcorn would lead!"

"Mentor," sighed Juliet. "I think we should let Sherman go home."

"That's the first sensible thing you've said since I arrived," she declared.

I stood up. The bed vanished and the white room reshaped into a chamber with a window, which I walked sheepishly towards.

"See you at school, Juliet?" I uttered.

She gave me a resigned wave, but it wasn't one of commitment.

I slid back down the ship's tripod leg and landed on the lawn with a hard thump.

Just like my love life.

CHAPTER TWENTY-SEVEN

Second Chance at a Second Chance

I drifted home to find Dad in the living room, slumped on the sofa, staring at the television. It was off. I stood behind him. In the reflection of the black screen, I could see that he was crying. My dad didn't do emotions. He did commands, hierarchy and discipline. But here he was, sitting alone, in tears.

"Dad?" I asked. "Are you okay?"

"I just miss her so much," he said, wiping his sniffle on his shirtsleeve. I slipped onto the sofa beside him and spotted an empty DVD container on the coffee table. It was their wedding video.

"I know," I said. "I do too."

"And I'd give anything to see her just one more time."

That gave me the chills.

"I know, I know, it's impossible," he sighed. "But I need her help, for you and Jess; I need to know how she did it. How come she was so great with you two and I'm just, well . . . I'm clearly doing something wrong."

Now was not the time to list Dad's parental shortcomings (though I'd start with: strict, emotionally unavailable, not prepared to listen, workaholism, favoring Jess) so I simply said, "It's not the same without her. But maybe it'd help if you listened a bit more."

He tore his gaze from the blank TV and looked at me.

"I'm listening," he said.

Now was my chance. "Like when I tell you there's a planet-ending invasion on its way—"

"Sherman, not this again! I don't know if this is you crying out for attention, but to slander an alien race that the Bureau considers an ally is not mature."

"But, Dad, it's—"

And then he sent me to my room, which was never much of a punishment since I could happily entertain myself for hours in a Jessica-free environment.

But I got myself ready for bed and lay awake, my head turning over the day's events. I'd flown a rocket ship for the first time and met my dead mother. It wasn't just an average Saturday. I regretted trying to warn Dad again, because for a moment we were actually on the cusp of having a real conversation. Eventually I drifted off to sleep, but soon afterwards was stirred by a familiar blue glow.

Juliet was hovering at the foot of my bed.

Was I dreaming?

"Hello, Sherman," she said. "I like your rocket collection."

She was admiring the display of the Saturn models on my bookshelf. They were in order of mission, of course.

"What are you doing here?"

"I came to apologize for tonight."

"No, I should apologize about the drive-in first," I said.

"There's no need. NED told me everything."

"What? What did he say?"

"He explained that you were embarrassed to be seen with me," she said. "I was hurt, and it would have been nice if you'd been able to tell me in person, but I understand."

"NED lied," I said. I couldn't believe someone so omnipotent couldn't see the obvious.

"Deities don't lie."

"This one does. He's dead wrong," I said, then took a deep breath – this was my chance. "I like seeing you and being seen with you, in fact I love it. Juliet, you've turned Drama from my least favorite subject to my most favorite subject. You literally brighten my day when I see you and I don't mean just with your glow."

"Really?"

"Yes, really. I didn't strand you at the drive-in on purpose. I was jumped at the snack bar and thrown into a garbage container."

"You were playing sports instead of being with me?"

"No, getting trashed is not a sport. Well, not that I know of. It's just stupid bullying that happens everywhere and that ruined our date. But I like you so much that I'm risking life in a Russian gulag by racing in the rocket trials tomorrow just . . . just to get you to notice me."

"I do notice you, Sherman," she said. "That's why I was so hurt."

"I'm sorry," I said. And I explained about Germany, my rocket and the threat of being extradited to Russia.

"Are you scared of breaking the rules?" she asked.

"I figure it's worth it," I said.

"Okay, I'll be there to cheer you on," she said. "I'm glad we're friends again, Sherman."

She dematerialized, leaving that one, heart-breaking word hanging in the air.

Friends.

Uh oh.

Now I was stranded.

In the friend zone.

CHAPTER TWENTY-EIGHT

The Vortex of the Friend Zone

The race trials were late on Sunday night. Officially, everyone was welcome to enter the Rocket Races, but the Groom Lake students had a long-standing, secret selection process – a series of midnight drag races to select the competitors. As my friends and I gathered at the hangar once our parents went to sleep, I knew this was my moment to make it to the show.

"Are you sure she used the F word?" asked Sonya.

I recounted the whole conversation, from Juliet materializing in my bedroom ("Hot!" said Octo) to vanishing after saying she was happy to be friends again ("So not hot!").

"You're in the friend zone," sighed Sonya.

"Anyway, she's not even allowed to date non-deities," I added.

"She may be a deity," Octo said, "but she's a teenager. Have faith in her instinct to rebel!"

"But for now," said Sonya, "focus on qualifying for the race finals."

"By my calculations," said Houston, "competing in the Rocket Races is your optimal path out of the friend zone."

"And, not to be down on Sherman's ace piloting skills," Octo said, "but I've got a little advantage up my sleeve. Well, technically, wrapped around my sleeve. Well, okay, so I don't wear sleeves, but get a load of *this*."

He took off one of his sports charities rubber bracelets, a yellow one. As I wondered if Lance Armstrong was any relation to Neil Armstrong, Octo stretched it open like an elastic band – to the size of a hula-hoop.

Inside was a swirling black hole.

"What is that?" I asked, staring into a vortex of space.

"It's a wormhole conduit," he explained. He took off and opened another bracelet, red this time, and stuck a tentacle through it. Immediately, the tentacle disappeared inside the red-ringed vortex and popped out of the yellow hoop.

"We ventitents invented the technology, and we've got the patent."

"But what does this mean . . . ?" Sonya began, but then figured out exactly what Octo was suggesting, just as we all did.

"So you want me to cheat?" I asked.

"It would certainly guarantee victory," said Houston.

"But it's cheating, guys," I protested. "The whole point of this is to impress Juliet, not to make her think I'm a no-good cheat." It was tempting, but I had to do this for real. "No, I'm sorry. Good intentions, Octo, but let's keep wormholes out of this race and qualify fair and square."

"Okay, buckaroo," said Octo. "I understand." He closed the vortices and slipped the bracelets back on his tentacles. "But the offer will always be there."

I got suited up into Aldrin and we moved the rocket out of the hangar to the drive-in, which, at the edge of the salt flats, was serving as the starting area.

The race trials were at midnight, under a breath-takingly full moon and a billion stars. The movie screen was dark and the concession stand closed, but there was a big crowd assembled to watch the qualifying. The space-cars – instead of being lined up in rows to watch a movie – were arranged in a giant crescent shape, blasting music and shining their headlights on a revving, roaring collection of nine rocket racers getting checked by their crews.

Atawee was there, clicking his claws and polishing the same red, Ferrari-style rocket he showed off at the drive-in.

"Why's he racing?" I asked Octo. "I thought he was sponsoring me."

Octo laughed. "Don't know a lot of scorps, do ya? They pierce for the kill and hedge their bets."

Klaatu and his pit-crew of three other Martians bickered as they inspected a sleek, UFO-type saucer. Klaatu's cousin Irwoot was racing in another heat, and I detected some distinct family tension. Three Xenophine Reeds dropped glowing green cubes into what I guessed was the fuel tank of their yellow, spherical racing-pod. Their pilot contorted himself through a small hole in the sphere, disappearing inside to take control.

I scanned the crowd for Juliet, and finally spotted her blue glow beside NED. Of course. He was marrying stock, after all.

"She's here," I said.

"Good," said Octo. "You show her what you're made of and race yourself out of the friend zone."

I also noticed Jessica – chatting with an insect-type in

a backwards baseball cap – and realized we'd *both* snuck out of the house tonight.

Dad was snoring away, in an empty house.

"I instigated the rumour as planned," Houston announced. "The crowd believes you are my brother Aldrin, and that you're here as a new exchange student."

"Good one, Houston," Sonya said. "Now c'mon, boys, we're in the first heat."

The four of us rolled the rocket out of the drive-in's gate. The crowd pressed up to the fence behind us, pointing their phones to take photos.

"You've been drawn against the Reeds," Sonya said as she pushed, "and a Yazzerbeast called Batta."

"Yazzerbeast?" I asked. "Like Graz?"

"Same species, meaner outlook," Houston confirmed.

"Great," I groaned.

At the starting line – a blackened trough lasered into the dirt by an AJABot – three Slugs in glowing yellow tunics yanked the racer out of our hands and carefully positioned it between the Reed's sphere and Batta's rocket. Then Octo wrapped a few tentacles around me and lifted me into the pilot seat.

This was it.

I had to win my heat to qualify.

No pressure then.

CHAPTER TWENTY-NINE

Trial by Rocket

I grabbed the wheel and the virtual dashboard flashed to life. The racer could feel me. It knew what I wanted. And what I wanted was . . . to win.

Sonya called up to me from the tarmac.

"You can beat the Reeds on speed," she said, "but against a Yazzerbeast, you'll have to be cunning. Try to annoy him. Use his temper against him. Break his concentration."

Batta's racer looked like a hundred bazookas glued together then spray-painted black. He snarled at me from his cockpit. He was smaller than Graz, more wiry. But he had sharper teeth and a scarier growl.

I waved, cool as I could, trying to unnerve him.

The Slugs ushered my friends back behind the fence, and I was suddenly alone with my frantically pounding heart.

Four AJABots glided over everyone's heads and hovered – gassy-smelling blue flames spurting from jets on their feet – above the starting line.

"Bipeds and quadrupeds, mammals and machines," the biggest one boomed, "welcome to the qualifiers!"

He explained the course was straight to the east radar tower and back – two hundred miles each way – and there would be three heats. Only the three winners would advance to the finals.

The drive-in screen burst to life with shaky images of the Reed, Batta and me, and then (when two of the AJABots whizzed way up into the night sky) it showed spectacular overhead views of the drive-in, crowd and racers.

"We're *filming* everything!" the loud AJABot said. "So you guys won't miss a *thing*!"

The crowd whooped and cheered.

"You there, Houston?" I said.

"I'm here," he said, his voice crackling in my ear. "They're going to start any moment. Get ready."

"Don't crash into the radar tower," Sonya's voice said.

"Do the spinning thing again," Octo said. "I can film it off the drive-in screen this time, buddy."

"*Don't* do the spinning thing," Sonya said.

"RACERS . . . " the AJABot announced, louder than ever, "are you READY . . . ?"

Batta punched the air and howled.

The yellow sphere shimmered and went transparent. The Xenophile pilot inside waved with his whole body. The crowd loved it.

I gave another thumbs-up. Pressed the clutch with my left foot. Hovered my right foot over the accelerator.

"Remember, Sherman," Houston said. "*Gently.*"

"RACERS . . . " the AJABot continued, "five . . . four . . . three . . . two . . . ONE . . . "

I hovered my foot over the accelerator.

"*IGNITION!*"

I stomped as hard as I could, shooting off like, well, you know, a rocket.

"GENTLY!" Sonya yelled.

"Keep the radar tower in sight," Houston said. "You *must* be ready for your turn."

"Spin it!" Octo growled.

The air *whooshed,* the giants in the engines did their teeth-rattling "AAAAAAAH" thing, and I lined up my trajectory with the floodlit tower in the distance.

I checked my flanks. I was keeping pace with the other two rockets.

"Hey," Octo said in my earpiece, "nice *going*, Earthman! Show him, Houston!"

A floating TV picture *bleeped* into life and showed me three dazzling white lines – the racers' three exhaust flames – shooting across the desert.

And the middle one, my rocket, was in the lead.

"Don't get too excited," Sonya said. "Anytime now that yellow ball's gonna . . . "

There was a yellow flash to my left, and the sphere roared. On the screen, the Reed's vapour trail suddenly drifted upward, above Batta and me.

" . . . start having fun."

"He's gonna loop!" Octo laughed. "Then bounce."

Over the intercom, I heard the drive-in crowd start chanting.

"Loop de loop . . . loop de loop . . . loop de loop!"

Then it happened. The yellow sphere soared up, up, up towards the stars, then swooped back down, bouncing off the desert floor like a rubber ball and hurling through the air until it was right back next to me.

Batta, meanwhile, had made up some ground and was close enough for me to see a long, gloopy string of Yazzerbeast snot fly from his nose and splatter against his racer's steering fins.

Classy.

"Any tips from the pit crew?" I called.

"Go-uh fas-uh-ter, dude," Octo said, clearly chomping something at the same time. "You need to go faster."

"Tell the ventitent," I said to Houston, "to just enjoy his pizza. I'm going flat-out here."

"He says to just enjoy your pizza," Houston said.

"Whoa," Octo marveled, "how did he know it was pizza?"

"Will you guys *concentrate*?" Sonya said. "The tower's coming up, Sherman."

The Reed was on my port side and Batta to my starboard. We were neck and neck and neck. Suddenly, Batta rammed into me.

"Argh!" I yelled. The rocket races were supposed to be non-contact, but then again, so was "touch" football.

The bump sent me into a spiral, and I pulled the ship up to avoid hitting the yellow ball. Once I was upside down, I spotted Batta's ship careen across – and smash sideways into the unsuspecting Reed ship. It bounced uncontrollably across the ground.

My competitors were down . . . but I was in a death spiral, and I couldn't stop.

I spun and spun, unable to regain control.

"Your starboard engine's malfunctioned," said Houston. "It's keeping you in the spiral."

"You've got to jettison it," said Sonya.

I opened the hood to the two levers that controlled the rocket boosters. I pulled up hard on the right-hand lever, but nothing happened.

"It's stuck," I screamed, going into another spin.

"Sherman, watch the tower!" called Sonya. "Don't hit it!"

That was it! I could knock the dud rocket off the racer by clipping the tower.

I controlled the spiral just long enough to slam my starboard rocket into the concrete tower, dislodging it from the racer.

I heard a *CRUNCHHHHHH* as the engine slammed off.

"Good move!" cried Octo.

I swung the ship around and prepared to race to the finish – not that I had any other rocket to worry about now. It was then I noticed that not only had I knocked off my own misfiring rocket, I'd fractured the tower. It was collapsing like an oversized game of Jenga.

"Move it!" shouted Sonya.

I hit the acceleration, hoping to avoid any falling concrete, and blasted my way back across the dark desert.

I shot over Batta yelling at the Reed, who was twisted into a pretzel but fortunately not hurt.

I eased up on the engine, worried about overheating the single fusion booster, and soon soared triumphantly over the finish line. The crowd cheered and I heard the AJABots announce Aldrin as the winner, advancing me to the finals.

At that moment, I wanted to rip off the mask and get some credit for what had been a pretty eventful race, but I knew if I did, NATO would be handing me over faster than I could say Article Five.

I parked the rocket away from the crowds, behind the drive-in screen, and Octo reached up with a few tentacles to lift me to the ground.

We hugged, high-fived, and whoo-hooed.

My whole body buzzed with excitement. I felt part of something, a team . . . a *winning* team.

"You did great, Sherman," said Sonya.

"Good flying," said Houston. "For a human."

"Thanks, guys." I scanned the distant crowd, looking for the blue glow. But both Juliet and NED were gone. "Did she stay to see me win?"

"Dunno," Octo said. "We were all eyes on you, buckaroo."

CHAPTER THIRTY

Dressing the Part

With the race trials behind me, and both the Rocket Race final and Prom three weeks away, I turned my attention from Groom Lake to fair Verona, *where we lay this scene.*

It was a Friday, and Drama was the first class of the day, and our last rehearsal before the big show that night. While everyone else gossiped and texted before class began, I quietly snuck into the back corner of the auditorium and tried to concentrate on running my lines.

But as soon as I started repeating, *"A greater power than we can contradict Hath thwarted our intents,"* to myself, the whole place went completely, utterly silent. And when I looked up – expecting to see Ms Teg watching us from the doorway – what I saw was Juliet walking into the room.

Walking.

Not floating.

And the glow was gone too. I mean, believe me, the girl still *glowed*. No beams of light any more, it was just . . . her, a teenage girl, but she could totally *teach the torches to burn bright*.

Her hair was light brown, in a loose ponytail. She wore ripped jeans, and a really cool faded gray T-shirt with a little Saturn logo on the front. She paced self-consciously past the staring Xenophine Reeds and Slugs and AJABots and Aristox as they watched her – every inch of the way – walk down the aisle, slink along my row, and take the seat next to me.

And it was only once she'd given the room a little wave that, slowly, everyone got back to their phones and their conversations.

"I can't believe it's you," I said. "You look so . . . human."

"What can I say? I'm a disciple of the Method."

"Aren't you going to get in trouble for taking physical form on this 'primitive planet'?"

"Probably. But I figured if you'd risk getting imprisoned just to get my attention, the least I could do is show up for the play in the right costume."

A sudden shudder shook through me. I had to ask.

"You didn't, um, *clone* this look from someone else, did you?"

"No, this is all me." She took the band out of her hair and swung her head to the side. Her hair caught the light and swooshed like in a shampoo ad. I was mesmerized.

Octo gyroscoped up to the two of us, and nodded. "Nice look. I think Sherman's got something he wants to ask you."

I wasn't ready for the big proposal, but I knew what Octo was thinking. Since Prom night coincided with the NED invasion, keeping Juliet around in physical form was our best chance of ensuring our planetary bodyguard would be on Earth when the NEDs arrived.

Octo moved down towards the stage, reciting his Mercutio lines, leaving me to prematurely pop the big question. The fate of the world rested on my narrow shoulders.

"Juliet," I said, finally mustering the courage. "Would you go to the Prom with me?"

She looked at me.

Up, down, and all over. I wasn't sure if she was sizing me up, or figuring out how to let me down. Then she smiled.

"I wasn't sure if you'd ever ask, Sherman," she said. A look of confused horror must have crept across my face because she added quickly, "Yes, I'd love to go."

"With me, right?"

"Yes, with you."

I couldn't believe it, even though I knew it was happening. It felt so, well, un-Sherman-like. It looked like I really was going to save the planet and acquire the hottest Prom date at the same time.

"Thespians, first positions please," called Ms Teg, fluttering into the auditorium. "Final rehearsal before our big night."

*　*　*

It's amazing how easy everything seems when you're walking on sunshine. Juliet and I killed it in rehearsal. Then I aced a popquiz in Planetology, and even nailed the problem set in Math class. So by the time I reassembled with my crew at lunch, I was feeling a million per cent.

The cafeteria was as packed and crazy-smelling as always, and most of the chatter – audible in between the crashing plates and chanting football players and hollering lunch ladies – was about Aldrin. Houston's mysterious brother, who beat the Reed and the Yazzerbeast into the race finals, hadn't been seen since the trials. Absence, it seemed, made Groom Lake's gossip mill grow curious.

"Sherman!" Octo hissed, munching on a Sentuviah eyeburger and slurping root beer through a straw. "Don't look now, bro, but Juliet has entered the cafeteria . . . she's grabbed some food from Nancy aaaaaand . . . she's a-comin' this way!"

I crossed my fingers under the table, secretly hoping she'd want to break the strict social hierarchy of the cafeteria's caste system. But I knew that she had a rep to protect. And thanks to the gulag-avoiding robotic disguise, I was still just Sherman Capote to the masses.

Sonya licked three tonguefuls of Venusian mouse-mousse from her spoon. "Juliet's the queen bee of the cool table, Sherman," she said. "I doubt she'll lower herself."

I tried to keep it cool.

Mr Cool.

Señor Suave.

Monsieur Mojo.

Lord Lowkey.

I did my best to focus on not spilling gravy on my favorite NASA T-shirt, but from the corner of my eye I kept track of her new human-look as Juliet shimmied between tables, still heading our way, balancing her tray and ignoring cat-calls from the Fungi.

"Besides," Sonya went on, "if she *does* sit here, it's only gonna attract awkward questions. Everyone thinks Aldrin's the big hero, remember. Not Romeo Capote here."

"She's not Aldrin's *Prom date* though," I said, grinning like an idiot.

Houston looked up from the racer blueprints he was scribbling on, checked no one would overhear, then whispered across the table.

"Everyone wants the nine-one-one on Aldrin," Houston said.

"Four-one-one," I corrected him.

"Does an omnipotent gal like Juliet actually *need* lunch?" Octo mused. "Isn't she just, like, powered by the cosmos?"

"Maybe not," I said, arranging my fries into a log cabin, "but she's here to experience normal life, isn't she? Maybe that includes the three-square-meals-a-day part."

"Thirty-three, dude," Octo said.

"I said *normal* life, not the all-you-can-eat-buffet life."

"In that case," Houston said, "I suggest we commence acting normal. My perimeter sensors indicate Juliet will be at this table in T-minus eight seconds . . . seven . . . "

"Whoa," Octo yelled, "you see the look on NEDster's face when she just strolled past the cool seniors' table?"

"*Shhh* your beaks," I whispered. "She's coming."

" . . . three . . . two . . . one!"

"Hi, Sherman, can I join you?" Juliet asked.

Her tray was filled with nothing but chocolate: chocolate bars, chocolate cake and chocolate milk.

"Since you've brought dessert for all of us," said Octo, "you can sit anywhere you like!"

"This one's free," I said, offering her the chair next to me. "What's with the cocoa-flavoured lunch?"

"You going on an un-health kick?" asked Sonya.

Houston's eyes glowed. "I've just scanned the contents of your tray and the total calories represent twenty-two thousand per cent of your recommended intake," he said.

"I've never had chocolate," confessed Juliet. "So I thought if I'm going to break a few rules, why not break a few more?"

"The Mentor doesn't know?" I asked.

"A girl who lives dangerously with her grub," laughed Octo. "I like her more already."

"I snuck out early this morning," Juliet said, with a giddy smile.

I caught Sonya rolling her eyes. "It'll make you fat, you know."

"I should try that too!" said Juliet, excitedly. "I've never been fat – what's it like?" She looked at Octo innocently.

"No, no, see this is blubber, not fat," he argued. "Big difference."

"Oh," said Juliet. "Well, you have lovely blubber."

Octo beamed from all three beaks.

"So, Juliet," started Sonya. "What brings you to the not-so-cool table?"

"I thought maybe Sherman and I should run lines one more time before tonight's performance. Will all of you be coming?"

Sonya grinned and draped an arm over my shoulder.

"To watch Sherman prance around in tights while Octo dies?" Sonya said. "We wouldn't miss it for the world."

CHAPTER THIRTY-ONE

Places Please

Word had spread that afternoon about Juliet and me being Prom dates, resulting in a strange combination of awestruck looks and jealous high-fives when I'd walked the halls between classes. Of course, most of the student body had appendages with anything but four fingers and a thumb, so "high-five" was more like high-claw or high-paw.

That night, the auditorium was sweaty and packed, and not just with students. When Juliet and I held hands and took our bows, the whole place – even the rest of the cast behind us – went wild. I spied Mr Meltzer, Mr Zvisst, Mr Orson and even Lunch Lady Nancy, all clapping away. Mrs Rackles didn't have hands, but I'm pretty sure that ear was cheering in her own way.

Even Dad was there, politely applauding in his civvies. Jessica had been great as Lady Capulet (maybe because Lady Capulet is distant, moody and annoying), and I'd nailed every scene I was in – but I wondered if Dad was actually proud or just clapping to feign parental supportiveness.

And when Juliet – to whoops and cheers from the crowd – surprised me with a kiss on the cheek, I wondered if she was enjoying Earth-life enough to *definitely* not disappear between then and the Prom.

I couldn't stop grinning. The applause and cheering kind of made up for Aldrin getting the credit for the race trials. And when we got a standing ovation, I have to confess, it boosted my ego to a new level. I may have been an anonymous racer-boy, but that night on stage, I became a school celebrity.

My cheek still tingling with Juliet's first kiss, I felt that finally everything was going to be okay. I would race the final Rocket Races, prove my awesomeness to Juliet and sweep her off her feet at Prom. When the NED invasion came, her physical presence on Earth would be the ultimate deterrent. Surely the NEDs wouldn't mess with an Icon.

Even Jessica gave me the slightest of approving head-nods from the wings and mouthed, *Bravo*.

For one moment, life couldn't get any better.

Until it got unimaginably worse.

"Get off that stage, young lady!" shouted my mom's

voice above the applause. The Mentor stormed down the aisle and jumped onto the stage with fists clenched and eyes glaring.

"A boy!" she yelled.

"Do you *mind*, madam?" Ms Teg squealed, fluttering in front of the rampaging Mentor. "Groom Lake High has a zero-tolerance policy toward pushy stage-moms!"

"I'm nobody's mother. I am the—"

"Mentor!" Juliet yelled. "What are you doing?"

The applause faded and a nervous, shocked alien babble rose up to replace it.

"Madam, if you *please*," Ms Teg hissed again.

But the Mentor ignored her, stomped straight up to Juliet, yanked her away from me by the wrist, and started wagging her finger. Right there. Center stage.

"A boy!" she yelled again. "You took physical form on this primitive planet for a *boy*?"

"Mentor, please," Juliet said, "people are watching!"

"A mortal boy with no powers, no standing in the universe . . . in tights?"

"I don't usually dress like this," I said in my defense.

But she just kept on ranting, and then suddenly turned to jab her finger at *me*.

"You stay away from this Icon!" she said. "She is spoken for!"

"I'm still in training," Juliet snapped, suddenly crying, "and I am *not* spoken for."

"You *will* be, young lady. Your parents have ordered a Pairing!"

"What?!" cried Juliet, yanking back her wrist, hitching her costume away from her feet and storming off stage-right. "No!"

"Where do you think you're *going*?" called the Mentor, before turning back to me. "This is all *your* fault."

As if on cue, the spotlight swung onto me, half-blinding me. As I squinted through the light, I spotted Mr Meltzer shaking his head and rolling his eyes.

And then I saw Dad.

He was frozen. His mouth open. His eyes wide behind his glasses.

"CAROL!" he yelled, loud enough to silence the entire crowd.

It took a few moments for the Mentor to realize someone was talking to her. She shielded her eyes and gazed out from the stage.

"Carol!" Dad called again, quivering. "Is. That. Really. You?"

A lump came straight to my throat. I checked the wings for Jessica, and saw her sprawled on the floor, with Quudo crouched over her, fanning his limbs to cool her down.

I could only watch as Dad pushed through the crowd and scrambled up onstage. He stood there, frozen.

"You're . . . alive?" he whispered.

"Dad, listen," I said. "She's not . . . "

The Mentor narrowed her eyes. "I see," she said. "You must be—"

"This is my dad," I said to her.

"Of course," the Mentor said, and she gave Dad a kind of weak, you-poor-thing smile.

Dad grabbed her arms.

"You're *alive!*" he whispered again.

The Mentor wriggled gently out of his grip and started edging away, backwards, and offstage.

"Sherman," she said, "would you mind filling your father in on the details? I genuinely don't have time. I have a rebellious goddess *in-training* to reprimand and a Pairing to prepare for. You understand, I'm sure. *Teenagers.*"

And then, unbelievably, she was gone.

"It's not her, Dad," I said. "It's not Mom."

Dad gazed at me. Gazed offstage. Gazed at Jessica, who was now sitting up and sipping from a glass of water. He sighed a huge, desperately sad sigh.

"Then once again, son," he said, "it seems you have some serious explaining to do."

As the audience's attention moved away from us and they began filing out of the auditorium, I finally came clean about the rocket and Mom's ashes. Then I tried to explain the physics of the Mentor's intergalactic cloning, but Dad interrupted me. "You launched her ashes in that rocket?"

"I just wanted her to get her wings," I confessed. "She always wanted that, ever since she was young, and I figured this was her best chance to ever fly that high. It was something I could do for her. Only me. I know you don't understand, but this was just something *I* had to do . . . for her."

"You launched her ashes in that rocket?" he said, stuck on repeat.

"Yes, Dad, I just—"

"Without inviting me?"

And then he did the most un-Dad like thing he'd ever done.

He hugged me.

CHAPTER THIRTY-TWO

Star-Crossed

In the weeks that followed, Juliet – thankfully still in physical form – ignored me at school and the Mentor refused to let me aboard their ship.

In GalLang class, instead of conjugating verbs, I formulated conspiracy theories in the back row with Octo.

"What if she's finally realized that I'm no good for her?" I speculated. I secretly hoped she was simply ignoring me in order to keep on the Mentor's good side, but I knew that was probably naïve.

"That's why we stick to the plan," urged Octo. "You race the rocket, you win, you get your Prom date. You save the world."

Mrs Rackles, who could hear anything in a two-mile radius, interjected with some unsolicited dating advice – "To love is to suffer" – then punished us for talking in her class by forcing us to write out all of the tenses of "to love" and "to suffer" on the chalkboard. In French.

With twenty tentacles, it took Octo only a few seconds. Me, I was stuck at the board for ten minutes scrawling how I felt about Juliet in every tense. It was torture, but it gave me time to reflect.

Paternal relations had improved somewhat since the Mentor's shocking appearance. A few days after the disaster in Verona, Dad took Jess and me out for *What Beats a Pizza?* and we agreed a type of Capote peace accord. Jess was actually nice about my Romeo performance and I found it in my heart to compliment her on how good the Prom preparations were looking.

"There's only three of us in this squadron," Dad said, "and we Capotes have to stick together." Dad had a beer, Jess had fizzy water with lemon, and I indulged my cream soda fetish, and we toasted a fresh start at Groom Lake. Dad even proposed a toast to Mom.

"To Mom, and finally getting her wings," he said. "Thank you, Sherman, for doing that."

"Yeah," agreed Jess. "That was the coolest, stupidest thing you've ever done, but I'm glad she soared that high."

We finished our pizza and tucked into my favorite

ice cream, mint chocolate swirl. But the conversation turned as cold as the dessert as soon as I brought up the impending end of the world.

"In a way," I said, "I'm glad she's not here to witness *NED*ageddon."

"Sherman, you can't go around saying things like that about our allies," Dad warned. "The NED race is part of the Bureau and signatory to an intergalactic peace accord that has a very strict non-slander clause. You can't scaremonger like this."

Maybe I couldn't scaremonger, but I could still be scared.

* * *

I finally decided to confront Juliet about the cold shoulder. I couldn't take it any more – I needed to know whether we still had our Prom date.

As I approached the cool table, where Juliet was back in situ, Graz rose and muscled me back, growling, "COME FOR ANOTHER TRIP TO THE TRASH, SHER-MAN?"

With Earth's destruction just days away, I wasn't in the mood for Graz's gruff.

"It's Sherman," I said, "and I'm here to talk to my Prom date."

"She's spoken for," he growled.

I caught Juliet's eye and she gave me a look I'd never seen on her: helpless and resigned. Instead of radiant and confident, she seemed meek and defeated. NED casually stretched out his arm and put it around her. Juliet looked at me with sad eyes and shook her head. She was asking me not to make a scene.

I retreated from Graz and joined my crew at our table, announcing with new determination that we had to win the Rocket Race on Saturday. Not only could I not stand the sight of NED sidling up to Juliet, but now that I had a first-in-a-long-while glimpse of normal family life, I didn't want the world to end just when Dad was beginning to see me as a human being.

"You want to spend your *last week alive* stuck in the hangar?" asked Sonya.

"Why so negative, pinky?" said Octo.

"All is not lost," assured Houston. "I've been reviewing documentaries of Earth dating rituals and concluded that when the Earth male wins a major game or race, he invariably wins the girl."

"The *Earth* girl," snapped Sonya.

It was odd that Sonya was suddenly so negative, and Houston had become the optimistic one.

"Are you okay?" I asked Sonya.

She sighed, flicked her three tongues and shrugged it off as "family stuff".

"Which documentaries?" Octo asked Houston.

"Anthropological studies like *Grease*, *Teen Wolf*, *Footloose* and *High School Musical*."

He may have got the type of films confused, but he wasn't wrong. Winning that race was my last and best hope to win Juliet's heart. So I got them to agree to work every night on the rocket racer, making Carol ready for race day. Even if it meant spending possibly our last week alive in the hangar. At least I'd be doing it with friends.

CHAPTER THIRTY-THREE

Race for Your Life

Race day fell on the last Saturday of semester. It was Groom Lake tradition that the Rocket Race ran in the afternoon while Prom owned the evening.

The drive-in was like a summer carnival. Students, teachers and base workers of every species and origin mixed and mingled in the hot Nevada sun. They slid down giant inflatable waterslides, crashed bumper cars and lined up for sodas and hot dogs at the concession stand. Huge speakers on tripods blasted music and rhymed off rocketeer stats. A small fair was set up with alien twists on games of chance: plasma-ball, laser firing and a Zarkorian fish tank.

Of course, it was also the day we expected the NED attack, so I checked the crowd to see if Juliet was anywhere to be seen, and spotted her strolling around the fair with NED, eyeing the milk bottle game. But today I wasn't interested in games. I had a girl to impress and a world to save.

Two AJABots towed the racer from the drive-in to the start/finish line. Sonya and Houston walked alongside, asking me to check all the key instruments. For the finals, a much longer race, each racer was allowed to have a small onboard crew, and I was happy to have my friends along for the ride, even if Sonya was still in a funk.

"Where's that ventitent?" she asked. "He'd better not be late."

"There," I said, spotting him crouching at the start/finish line, scrounging in the sand. "What's he doing? Yoga?"

As our AJABots pulled us into position, Octo raced over and hauled himself up into the control cabin behind the cockpit.

"About time," Sonya snarled. "You finished playing sandcastles?"

"What's your *damage*, pinky?" Octo snapped back. "You've been a moody little lizard all week. And *today* you've done *nothing* but—"

"C'mon, guys," I said, "cool it, we need to focus."

I had my Victorian tuxedo on underneath the Aldrin suit, and planned to rush to Juliet right after taking the trophy. I'd swoop her away from NED, take her to Prom, and we'd dance the night away as the NEDs arrived to drain our planet of its magma. They'd realize there was an Icon habitating Planet Earth and they'd turn tail. I might even get a slow dance as a reward for my planet-saving brilliance.

It was all down to me, but strangely, I wasn't nervous. I was energized, excited, and like a young (and thin) John Travolta, ready to win the race and get the girl.

My crew climbed aboard as the two other racers lined up at the start/finish line. On our right was another team of Martians, led by Klatuu's cousin Irwoot, in a sleek, silver saucer. On our left was Graz, hoping to restore the Yazzerbeasts' honor after Batta's now infamous wipeout at the trials. Graz's racer appeared to replicate two truck-sized chainsaws bolted together. The thing looked utterly, utterly deadly.

Our course was an eight-hundred-mile loop from Groom Lake, around the Grand Canyon, and then back. First one home would be the winner. I was feeling pretty confident, thinking back to the two F-18s I outran in the canyon.

"All systems are go," said Houston through the intercom in my helmet.

The AJABots started the countdown: "Ten, nine, eight, seven . . . "

"Thanks for doing this, guys," I said. "It means a lot to me."

" . . . six . . . "

"Give it all you've got, Sherman," said Octo.

" . . . five, four . . . "

"Win it for all of us not cool enough to sit at the universe's cool table," said Sonya.

" . . . three, two, one . . . "

The bigger Bot fired the starting gun, which sounded like a small nuclear blast, and I slammed down hard on the accelerator. Both fusion engines roared as I raced across the salt flats, the world rushing by, Earth's destiny hanging in the balance.

Graz slammed towards my port side and I took to the sky, hoping to avoid his chainsaw. But he'd clearly learned from Batta and matched my altitude. I rotated on the horizontal axis, put the racer into a controlled, downward spiral and got clear of the immediate danger. But I sacrificed speed for safety. I pushed the fusion engines to their max. The ship vibrated violently.

"Please hold together . . . " I almost said "Mom".

"I'm working on getting you more power," called Sonya from the cabin. "I'm going to cut the air conditioning."

"Whoa," complained Octo, "let's not be hasty. There's always room for comfort."

By the time we reached the Grand Canyon, the sun was starting to set behind me and I was trailing in third position.

I brought the racer in low over the Colorado Plateau, miles of red, rocky desert, with spruce trees flashing by. I approached the rim and dived a mile deep into the grandest of canyons, spotting my competitors. Irwoot was in the lead, his engine's exhaust bathing Graz in blue light.

I caught myself distracted, just for a moment, by the breathtaking natural beauty of this place. The winding Colorado River sparkled at the base of the canyon and steep, jagged red rocks towered on either side. A flock of wading ducks sensed us approaching and had the good sense to migrate away at speed.

"This is one beautiful planet, buckaroo," Octo observed.

"Shame about the Yazzerbeast spoiling the view," I said, refocusing on the race. "I'm going to full thrusters to pass him. Sonya, do I have full power?"

"We're all set," she answered. "Boosters are primed."

"That's why it's so hot in here," huffed Octo.

I flexed my fingers on the wheel, prepared to overtake.

"Sherman, careful of his gravity blades," warned Houston. "They'll chew us up!"

"We're not going anywhere *near* them," I said. "Three . . . two . . . ONE!"

But the instant I made my move, the Yazzerbully extended a long pole that zapped with lightning.

Electric blue bolts fried our ship.

I was so focused on avoiding the deadly gravity blades, I hadn't counted on getting tasered. Sparks of electricity popped all over the hull and we sputtered and stalled. All I could do was guide us to a crash landing on the riverbed as Graz chased after the Martians through the canyon.

"You okay up there, pilot?" called Octo, opening the top hatch from the cabin.

"Besides the fact that we just got microwaved?"

"He shorted out the electrics," said Houston. "Our systems are sizzled."

"We've got to get back in the race," I called back in a panic. "Can you get us going?"

"We've got no power to start up the engines," Sonya lamented.

"So we're stuck?" I said, staring up the canyon wall, and up to the red sky. I thought about Theodore von

Kármán and his line between Earth's atmosphere and the rest of the solar system. I wondered if the rest of the solar system would miss Earth when it was gone.

For a moment, we sulked in silence. All I could hear were the waves lapping, and a few quacks from a brave duck that had returned.

"There is *one* way we can still win," Octo said with three smiles, "a *ventitentical* way."

We all knew he meant wormholes. But wormholes meant cheating.

"That's what you were doing," I realized, "at the finish line."

"You sneaky squidy," said Sonya. "You were setting up a wormhole conduit?"

"And I've got the corresponding one right here," boasted Octo, stretching out a pale green bracelet. We looked through time and space to see the cheering Groom Lake crowd glued to the images of the Martians racing across the desert.

"It'll instantly transport us to the finish line," he promised. "For the win!"

Sonya nodded in agreement. "And Graz has already cheated by electrocuting us."

It was so tempting.

"No," I said. "It's not the right way to win. We may

finish first, but it won't count for Juliet. Anyway, she's omnipotent – she'll know we cheated."

"There may be another way," offered Houston, climbing up into the cockpit. "But it's not without serious consequences."

"Is it legal?" I asked.

"Yes," said Houston. "There is an internal power source in Aldrin's suit, so, if I plug it into the main start-up capacitor, it would power—"

"Do it!" I shouted.

"Sherman, there will be consequences," he warned.

"Like the world ending?" I asked.

I didn't want to know about any consequences, just that it was possible to get back in the race and win Juliet's favor. I couldn't compete with NED's breeding, but I could compete on valor and honor.

Houston tethered the suit to the ship using a spare cord and the suit buzzed. The entire world felt electric. The ship powered up and I was ready to race.

"Okay," I said. "Let's finish this."

With my crew back in the cabin, I lifted off. I gave it everything I could. I lifted us out of the canyon and across the flat, sunset-bathed red desert sands.

"Thanks, Houston."

"Sherman, the suit is modulating the ship's power but the—"

"There's Irwoot," I shouted, seeing blue bolts dancing on the downed saucer. "Graz must've hit him too."

Now we just had to catch up to Graz. I could see the Yazzerbeast's racer in the distance. I looked at Carol's read-out – miraculously, it calculated that I could catch them with the fusion boosters at full power.

"Graz's fireworks must've drained his ship's power," I called to my team. "He's slowing down."

"Sherman—" started Houston.

"I know, I know, stay clear of his blades."

We soon caught up with Graz. I gave him a wide berth and blew past him, feeling triumphant.

"No, I—"

"Woohoo!" I shouted.

As we whooshed over the Arizona desert, racing back towards Area 51, I suddenly felt woozy, a bit like my first day at Groom Lake. My vision started to go spotty and I felt like all of my body hairs were being plucked out at once.

"I don't feel so well," I said, finding it hard to catch my breath. I tried to focus, and keep the racer straight and steady, but couldn't see straight. I was going to faint.

"That's the consequence," said Houston. "It's a side effect."

"Of what?" I asked, trying not to puke in the helmet.

"Digitization."

"What?" I gasped.

"Houston?" chirped Sonya. "What's happening to our pilot?"

"I had to reboot the ecto-suit to power the ship's start-up," explained Houston, as if it should mean something to me. "It automatically initiated the digitization process."

Digitization.

"You mean I'm being turned into a robot?!"

"Technically, your brain is being scanned right now, but once that's complete, yes, the suit will automatically cut and copy your gray matter onto the hard drive."

"And then what happens to my brain?" I yelled.

"It would be discarded, obviously, along with your redundant body. Just like me."

If the Aldrin suit got its way, I was soon to become a walking piece of hardware.

"No offence, Houston," I said, hoping he wouldn't take any, "but I really want to keep my brain and my body."

"Actually, buckaroo, metallic is a good look for you," Octo said.

"Swig some water, squidy," snapped Sonya.

"Houston, please," I begged. "Can you stop it?"

"Only by removing the suit, but then we'd lose power."

"And speed," I realized, as we hurled across the desert with Graz now in close pursuit. It looked like I might win the alien race, but lose my Earthly body. I'd be a computer in a robot's shell.

"How long do I have?" I asked. "Before I . . . "

"Not long," Houston said over the intercom. "Once the initial scan is complete, the digitization process cannot be reversed."

"How long?!" I screamed.

"About a minute," Houston said solemnly.

One minute. I had to cross the finish line in one minute. I had nothing against computers or robots per se, but I did not want to be one. My physical, organic body may have been smaller than average and still recovering from puberty, but at least it was mine, and I wanted to keep it. I also had a hunch that robots weren't Juliet's type.

"Guys, channel all available energy into the boosters," I ordered. "I'm going to make one final burst."

I tried to focus, but my vision was blurring.

"You're good to go, dude," Octo confirmed. "Punch it!"

"Come on, Carol," I whispered, before slamming down on the accelerator, kicking the ship into its highest gear. "Help me out."

We soared back to base and sailed over the finish line.

Victorious, but was it too late?

"It's started," I heard Houston sigh. "Hold on, Sherman!"

My brain felt like it was being suctioned out as the suit ripped at my consciousness. Everything went black, and in the darkness I saw a swirl of a million stars. I tried to hold onto reality, but as I passed out on the dashboard, I slipped into a vast nothingness.

I had won the race, but had I lost my body?

CHAPTER THIRTY-FOUR

Unmasked

In the darkness, I could hear the crowd cheering and applauding. The noise was faint at first, but slowly swelled like someone was turning up the volume dial. I opened my eyes, unsure if they were new robotic sensors or factory-issue hazel peepers, and saw Octo, Houston and Sonya standing over me. And then Juliet came into view.

"You did it, Sherman," she said softly.

They sat me up in the dust beside Carol, just over the finish line. The Aldrin suit was disassembled around me. In a daze, I moved my legs and arms, and rubbed my chest. Everything hurt, but it all felt organic, one hundred per cent . . . me.

"Am I . . . normal?"

"That's a loaded question, buckaroo," said Octo.

"We got the suit off just in time," said Houston. "Juliet helped."

I glanced up and spotted my face on the drive-in screen.

My face.

My *exposed* face.

Of course. The AJABots who'd been filming the race were covering this post-race drama, which meant my secret identity was a secret no more. The crowd chanted, "SHER-MAN, SHER-MAN!"

I hid my head in my hands, but I was much too late. I'd been outed as the victorious rocket racer. I wondered how long I had until NATO arrived to haul me away.

"Sherman?" asked Juliet, crouching down beside me. "You really risked the gulags – just to impress me?"

"Yeah," I muttered, my head still pounding from the brain scan.

"Well, I'm definitely impressed," she said. "And I'm definitely your Prom date."

"Really? But what about the Mentor, and your rules, and NED?"

"I think I needed to learn from you how to break the rules," she said. "Thank you."

I was still dizzy from the aborted digitization, which meant I had no filter between brain and mouth. I just blurted out the truth.

"I was so worried, Juliet, that you'd leave before

Prom, before the NEDs attacked, but you're here and you can bodyguard the Earth tonight—"

"*Bodyguard?*"

Juliet's eyes widened with rage and disappointment. And then I realized what I'd said, how it must've sounded to her.

"Is that why you asked me to Prom?" she asked. "So I'd *bodyguard* the planet?"

"No!" I said. "Well, yes, but—"

And then, she exploded.

Literally.

A globe of dazzling blue light burst from her and flashed across the drive-in, so bright it nearly blinded me. I looked away, shielding my eyes. When I finally looked back, she was just as luminescent as the first time I saw her materialize in Ms Teg's drama class. She was ethereal again, a bright blue light floating in the dusk and looking down at me with disdain and disgust.

"I thought you were *different*, Sherman Capote," she raged. "I thought – I hoped – that just *maybe* you liked me for who I am. Not for *what* I am."

She jumped into the air and hovered over me the way hawks circle over mice.

"Hey, douse the fireworks, bluebird," Octo called, "this guy really *digs* you."

"No, he doesn't!" Juliet cried. "He's as bad the rest! He's just using me because I'm an Icon. He's as bad as NED, worse even! At least NED doesn't try to hide it. I might as well go along with the *Pairing* if this is the way—"

"What Pairing?" I asked.

But before Juliet even began to explain, the pieces fell together. NED's text from his dad ("YOU'VE EARNED YOURSELF A PAIRING"), the Mentor's comments about the NEDs, Graz's comment in the cafeteria.

NED and Juliet. Paired.

"Our ceremony is tonight – on their planet," Juliet sobbed. "I was going to refuse, go to Prom with you, run away. But now . . . "

POOF, she disappeared.

Just like that, into thin air. She vanished from my life, and from Planet Earth.

And for a few moments, Octo, Houston and I just stared at each other, not knowing what to say, the AJABots capturing the entire episode on the big screen.

The silence was broken by Sonya, on the phone. Sobbing.

"Oh, hey," I said to her, "I'll be okay. But maybe don't go telling everyone I just got dumped."

"THIS ISN'T ABOUT YOU!" she yelled. "NOT EVERYTHING IS ABOUT SHERMAN CAPOTE!"

"What's with her?" I asked the guys.

She put away her phone and said, "I've been *Called*. My whole family has. We've been Called to perform our Balleropera at NED's Pairing. Tonight."

Not only was NED stealing my would-be girlfriend, he was summoning my best girl *friend*.

"And we're not ready," she said, solemnly. "I've been spending more time on the rocket than rehearsing. And if we make even one mistake in the recital . . . "

She didn't finish the sentence. She didn't need to. We all knew the punishment for imperfection.

And just when I thought it couldn't get any worse, I heard the sirens.

Four Military Police Jeeps revved into the finish area and surrounded us, blinding me with their spotlights.

"That's Sherman Capote," snarled an unwelcome, snobbish voice. "The rocket racer."

NED.

He'd led the cops straight to me.

The Military Police jumped from their Jeeps and rushed me. As Octo, Sonya and Houston protested, they forced me onto my knees, pulled my hands behind my back and tightened plastic handcuffs around my wrists.

NED stood over me and boasted, "Tonight I'll be Paired with Juliet, restoring order to the universe, and tomorrow I'll be sipping on the delicious remnants of your puny planet."

"You're a monster," I spat.

"I am a god," he snarled. "And the god always gets the girl."

His cape billowed in the non-existent wind as he strolled off into the darkness, leaving the police to hoist me into a waiting Jeep.

"By Article Five of the Geilenkirchen settlement," the officer monotoned, "you are hereby to be remanded to the Russian Federation."

NED got the girl, and I got the gulag.

CHAPTER THIRTY-FIVE

The Groom Lake
Redemption

I saw this prison movie once where the prisoner escaped by digging a tunnel behind a poster he'd put up in the cell. The poster was of Rita Hayworth, a beautiful movie star from the 1940s. She had wavy hair and was kneeling on a bed, smiling an old-fashioned Hollywood smile. It took the man nineteen years, scraping away with a little chisel, to dig his way to freedom. I'd been thinking about him for hours, because that exact poster was on the wall of my own cell.

I couldn't resist taking a peek underneath, but there was no tunnel. Instead, *NO REDEMPTION!* was scrawled in thick red marker pen on the cream-colored concrete.

Prison guards, I decided, had a warped sense of humor. I noticed a tiny spy-camera, filming me from the corner of the ceiling. I imagined a patrol of potbellied uniformed guards, clutching mugs of instant coffee and inhaling doughnuts, watching their screens and chuckling at the incarcerated rocket racer.

"Heads up, kid," a voice said.

I looked up to see a guard who looked about sixty, dressed in a green uniform so crisp it could give you a papercut, with muscles Graz would maim for. He swiped a keycard in the corridor and a loud *BUZZZZ* startled me. The metal bars slid open and I made the mistake of getting my hopes up.

"Am I getting out?" I asked.

"I don't think you're ever getting out, kid."

"Oh," I sighed, thinking I'd better start digging behind Rita.

"But you do have a visitor."

He motioned to someone I couldn't see, and I heard footsteps echo on the concrete. Then, my heart sinking faster than a Xentaurian mothership, I saw Dad. Standing there in rolled-up shirt sleeves, red-eyed and bristly-chinned. He held two ice-cream tubs in his hand.

"Ten minutes, Mr Capote," the guard said and strode off, fingers stuck in his belt like a sheriff.

Dad sat down next to me on the bed and handed me a tub.

"Don't get too excited, Sherman," he said. "It's just

ice cream. There's no key hidden in there or anything."

And you know what he did?

He actually smiled.

Instead of scolding me, lecturing me, or displaying his deep disappointment in me, he actually gave me a break. I peeled off the lid and gazed at the green and brown swirl. It was mint chocolate. My favorite.

"How did you know?"

"You think I don't know my boy's favorite ice cream?"

Honestly, I didn't.

I dug in with my little plastic spoon. It tasted of comfort. The flavor was an Air Force staple, available on bases around the world, and as a kid, it was always the one thing that comforted me after disappointing Dad on whatever sports field was popular in our host country. I'd slurped the swirl after rugby in England, baseball in Korea, tennis in France and soccer in Germany.

And yet today, not even the perfect blend of artificial mint and chocolate could comfort me.

"Dad," I said. "They're gonna send me to the gulag, aren't they?"

"I just don't know yet," he said. "This is all way, way above my pay grade."

"You could ask for a raise."

I turned my spoon upside-down, scraped some ice cream onto my tongue and let it melt in my mouth.

"What were you doing out there, son? You get banned by NATO from ever touching rockets and your response is to race one?"

"Two, technically," I said. "It was a double-fusion system so—"

"Sometimes I just don't understand you," he said. "You and Jessica are the two most important things in the universe to me, and yet sometimes you both seem so, I don't know, *alien* to me."

He still didn't sound angry, just really confused. So I braced myself, ignored the churning awkwardness in my stomach and told him about Juliet. About trying to impress her so she'd want to go to Prom with me. Then, I was about to try one last time to warn him about the NEDs when, for the second time in five minutes, Dad threw me a total curveball.

He started dishing out dating advice.

"Sherman, if that's how you feel about her," he said, "you have to tell her. Now. Before it's too late. I wish ... I wish I'd told your mother one last time before—"

"Time's up, Mr Capote," said the guard. "My boss'll be back in a minute and if I get caught—"

"Thank you, Gord," said my dad. "I appreciate you letting me see my boy."

"Don't mention it," replied Gord. He opened the bars with a *BUZZZ* and beckoned my father from the cell. "Seriously, don't mention it. To anyone. Oh, and by the way, I'm out of printer ink."

"Copy that," said Dad, rising and stepping into the corridor of freedom. "Oh, Sherman, I almost forgot."

He held out his hand and gave me a purple rubber bracelet.

"Your friend Octo gave this to me for you," Dad said. "Kind of weird present, guy-to-guy, but—"

Gord grabbed the bracelet. "I need to check that item," he said, rubbing it between fingers and thumb. I held my breath, hoping the guard had never seen a ventitent wormhole conduit before.

"It's a style statement," I lied.

"Well I wouldn't wear that in the big boys' lock-up," he warned, handing it back to my dad who slipped it onto my wrist. "But other'n that, it looks harmless enough."

"I'll come back for you, son," said Dad.

"Don't go anywhere, kid," quipped Gord, slamming the door behind them, and escorting my dad along the corridor – leaving me to plot my escape.

I tried to open the bracelet. It should have been easy but that was when I realized that ventitents were ridiculously strong. I tugged, yanked and pulled until I was lying back down, trying to expand the rubber with the force of my left foot.

I could just see the YouTube video now that the guards would post: me, squirming beneath a poster of Rita Hayworth, wrestling with a purple bracelet. At least if I failed, there wouldn't be anyone on Earth left to watch it.

I was still lying on the floor, feeling defeated, when a terrifying picture popped into my brain.

An almost-like-I-was-there, 3D-surround-sound image of Juliet gazing into NED's eyes, saying, "I do".

That did the trick. I gave the bracelet one almighty pull with both hands. It made a crackling sound followed by a low hum, and I was finally able to stretch it to the size of a hula-hoop.

I placed the vortex on the floor, blew Rita a kiss, and jumped.

Through the fabric of the universe.

CHAPTER THIRTY-SIX

Escape from Planet Earth

I couldn't tell which way was up.

Just an instant ago my shoes had been squeaking on concrete and now they were sliding around a kind of giant slithery catcher's mitt made of tentacles.

"I know it's cheatin', buddy," Octo said, "but I had to do somethin'."

As relieved as I was to be out of the prison, I did feel a little cheated.

"That was . . . "

"Disappointing?" Octo asked, putting me down on the floor of what appeared to be public toilets. "You were expecting a thrill-powered ride through a swirly-whirly vortex, right?"

I could hear a cheesy love ballad bellowing in the background. I looked around, trying to get my bearings.

"Don't think I'm not grateful, because I am. But where are we?"

"You shifted about half a mile, dude," Octo said.

Houston appeared from behind the ventitent, dressed as a merchant seaman and hauling the Aldrin suit's steel trunk.

"This is the gymnasium's male biological evacuation chamber," he said.

"Of course, school!" I said, finally recognizing the toilets as the ones attached to the locker room.

"We didn't want to draw attention to ourselves in case the cops were watching us," said Octo. "So we figured the can was the best place to hide."

"You know it's only girls who go to the bathroom together on this planet, right?"

"That's crazy," said Octo. "It's way more fun to pee in pairs."

"I prefer to change my oil in private," said Houston.

The ventitent peeled the bracelet off the graffitied tiles, shrinking it back to size and slipping it on the tip of his bare tentacle.

"Don't you need the other one?" I asked.

"Nah. If we collapse one side, it collapses the whole wormhole," he explained. "It takes two to tango."

Suddenly, the love ballad was drowned out by an air-raid siren. For a moment, I thought maybe it was Monday at ten o'clock and everything that had happened since I'd first arrived at Groom Lake had been just a dream. But dreams rarely smell of the boys' locker room.

"It's the NEDs," I said. "They're here. We've got to get Juliet back. Only she can stop this. Octo, can you zap us to the NED world?"

"If there was a corresponding bracelet already there, then yeah," he said. "I could zip us there straight away. But there's not."

"So we're stuck?" I said.

"We just gotta take the highway," he said. "There's a wormhole highway that runs straight past their planet. But we need to reach the on-ramp."

"Where's that?" I asked.

"Next to the moon," he said.

I looked up, spotted the envious moon glowing down on us.

"Sherman, do you really think Juliet will come back?" Houston asked.

"I don't know, but I have to try – and I have to tell her how I really feel."

"Technically the racer can break orbit," offered Houston.

"Let's go!" I announced.

Octo eyeballed me – those big rectangular pupils of his bulging a little – then he clamped his beaks together, which completely failed to stop a cephalopod guffaw bursting out and echoing all over.

"Good for you, Romeo!" he laughed, opening the toilet door with one of his tentacles. "Let's move, Metal Man. Let's do it for love, baby!"

We stepped into the gym – and were transported to a scene of science-fictional Victorian destruction. With dancing.

Three giant Martian war machines towered over the dance floor, suspending disco balls that shone stars all over the gym walls. Beneath the tripods, the costumed aliens slow-danced to Air Supply, I guess assuming the siren was just part of the *War of the Worlds* ambiance. I suddenly realized Octo was, as always, naked as the day he was spawned.

"Hey, buddy," I said to Octo, "no *War of the Worlds* costume?"

"According to H.G. Wells, I'm already dressed as a Martian."

"Got it."

"You think I've got time to ask your sister for a dance?" asked Octo.

My *sister*.

I spotted Jessica by the snack table, serving up Rilperdough and boxes of popcorn, and decided that if we were going off-world, I'd better take her with us in case my desperate plan failed.

"Jess, I'm so glad I found you." Even as I uttered the words, I couldn't quite believe I was saying them.

"What's going on, Sherman?" As Prom committee boss-supremo, she had this event choreographed down to the last detail, and her pale face told me she knew the siren wasn't part of the motif.

"It's the NED invasion," I said. "It's coming . . . and it's going to destroy the world!"

"Oh my god, Sherman. You ruin everything!"

"Come with us . . . that's if you ever want to plan another Prom!"

"I'm not going anywhere with—"

Octo scooped her up, pausing her protest, until she yelled, "Put me down, you . . . you . . . GROSSOPUS!"

I grabbed a box of golden popcorn from the snack table and followed Octo into the main hallway, then out onto the moonlit steps of Groom Lake High. Up above, a giant fire burned in the night sky.

It had to be the NED ship, coming into the atmosphere.

"What is that?" whispered Jess.

"That's what I've been warning Dad about," I said. "And we've got to stop it."

We piled into Octo's Toyota and he revved us through the chaotic streets of Area 51 to our hangar. Octo had to scale pavements to avoid hitting military vehicles scurrying around the streets – all of the adults had clearly been called into work.

"It's ventitent, not grossopus," Octo complained. "Not octopus, either. How many more times, people?"

Above Groom Lake, the ship stopped burning and finally came into view. It was a massive isosceles triangle, blacking out the stars.

"It's reached our atmosphere," I said.

Houston focused his optical receptors, scanning the shape.

"It's the tanker," he confirmed. "The same one that destroyed my planet. My receptors tell me it's big enough to hold ninety-eight-point-two per cent of the Earth's magma."

"I mean," Octo went on, "no matter how cute she is, a gal should try to get a guy's species right, you know?"

"OCTO!" I yelled. "Focus!"

With a booming, ultra-deep groaning sound that rumbled vibrations in my chest, a massive tube protruded from the belly of the spaceship and telescoped down towards the desert.

"What's it doing?" Jess shouted.

"That," Houston said gravely, "is the Magma Extractor."

"A giant straw, baby-cakes," Octo clarified.

"Don't call me baby-cakes," Jessica said. "And Sherman, does this mean all that invasion garbage you've been hassling Dad with is . . . true?"

"One hundred per cent true," I said. "And you know what else? The only way we're gonna survive is if I win back Juliet."

"So we're doomed," Jessica groaned.

"Thanks for the encouragement, sis."

By the time we reached the hangar the ground was shaking and sirens were blaring all over the base. I strapped myself into the cockpit and fired up the engine, as my crew piled into the cabin. All except Jessica.

"Jess!" I called over the engines. "Get in, please?"

"I'm not going near that thing," she said. "Can't you just let the Air Force handle this? I'm sure—"

A thunderous earthquake shook the hangar, sending tools rattling off the bench, corrugated iron panels crashing from the roof and Jessica tumbling backwards in her Victorian frock.

"Great, I've got dust all over—"

I could tell Jessica was really scared because she didn't make a sound, didn't even complain at all when Octo lifted her into the cabin.

I guided Carol towards the open door as the girders clanged onto the concrete all around us. I heard the scraping and screeching of tortured metal as the whole building was twisted out of shape behind us.

It was now or never. I had to win back Juliet or there wouldn't be any planet to come home to.

"Hit the gas, Romeo," Octo said, strapping himself into his seat.

I revved us out of the hangar and lifted us up into the air, just in time to see the hangar collapse from the tremors. Gazing down, something else struck me. Sonya's Eggcraft was gone too.

My first instinct was relief that at least she was off-planet and would be safe, but then I remembered why she was off-planet. The Balleropera ritual.

With Houston's navigation, I aimed for the stars and flashed the boosters.

"The wormhole on-ramp is just this side of the moon," said Octo. Houston calculated the trajectory and I did my best to fly straight.

As we soared past the massive tanker dominating the

night sky, it was obvious it had a one-track mind for magma – it took no notice of us. I let out a sigh of relief. We flew past the immense black triangle, on our way to win back the Icon who could save the planet from its destruction.

CHAPTER THIRTY-SEVEN

Invading the NED World

As we cleared the atmosphere, I realized I was now in a very exclusive club: humans who'd slipped the surly bonds of Earth.

I thought of all the astronauts who'd made this journey before me. I was well past the Kármán Line and I thought of the men and women who'd died in this pursuit. The Apollo 1 astronauts who didn't survive the launch pad, the Challenger crew who never made it to the Kármán Line, the Columbia astronauts thinking they were returning safely home, and of course George Clooney (no thanks to Sandra Bullock). As we were about to crash the royal wedding of intergalactic deities, I wondered if our fate was written in the stars.

"There it is," said Houston. "Just follow the trajectory."

It was invisible to the human eye, but Carol's digital

read-outs detected the anomaly – it looked like a plughole drain against the starscape.

"Ease off the throttle, buckaroo," said Octo. "Take those hand-thingies of yours off the wheel, and the vortex'll just suck us in."

"Got it," I said, secretly hoping he wasn't sending us into a black hole of doom.

"The what'll do what?!" Jessica blurted.

"It's cool, baby-cakes."

"Octo, don't ever call me b—"

Suddenly the stars spun as we were sucked down the plughole drain of the galaxy. At first, there was only the silence of the spinning stars, but pretty quickly the negative space of the wormhole filled with Houston, Octo and Jessica's screams. Like tourists on a rollercoaster.

"HERE C-C-COMES THE S-S-SWIRLINESS, B-B-BUCKAROO!!!"

The ventitent hadn't been kidding. This was what traversing space and time should feel like: a breathtaking multi-colored space whirlpool whooshing into existence, yanking us along a zillion twists and turns with my heart somewhere in my throat.

"S-S-SPIN IT!" Octo said.

"S-S-SPIN YOURSELF, OCTOPUS!" Jessica replied.

We were going so fast I couldn't think straight, let alone pull off aerobatics. I was overwhelmed by the star-lights swirling by, G-force pinning me to my seat, until I saw it: a smaller vortex ahead in the whirlpool's wall.

"TH-TH-THAT'S OUR EXIT, DUDE!" Octo yelled. "RIGHT TURN! RIGHT TURN!"

I nudged the wheel to starboard and zipped Carol through the opening. Instantly the wormhole whooshed out of existence and we were back in normal space – above a massive, dazzling, white-and-blue planet that made Earth look like a marble.

"Nice flyin', Sherman," said Octo. "Welcome to the NED world, everyone."

It looked – from fifty thousand feet, at least – kind of like Earth would look if someone painted all the continents eggshell white. The sky and ocean were blue as could be, but everything else had a white, matte finish.

"What's with all the glaciers?" I asked.

"It's Argosian megamarble," said Houston. "And those are not glaciers, they are shopping precincts."

"Shopping?" asked Jessica.

"Their planet," Octo explained, "is basically one massive series of interconnected shopping malls."

"How do you know?" Jessica asked.

"Am I the only one who pays attention in school?" huffed Octo.

I took us down until we were skimming waves and speeding towards the shore. Octo stretched his tentacles above his head.

"Not so low, Romeo!"

"Can't you swim?" Jessica asked.

"I'm allergic to water."

"An octop— sorry, a ventitent who's allergic to water?" Jessica laughed. "So what happens if you get wet?"

"Well . . . er . . . it starts off feelin' kinda sunburny, then . . . ah . . . some wicked dizzy spells kick in, followed by tingly tentacles, beak tremors, pop eye, puckered sucker syndrome – that kinda thing. After that, my skin starts to boil and if I'm really unlucky, you know . . . my hearts'll explode."

"Gross," she said.

"Too much information?" asked Octo.

I flew us towards a glistening sandy beach lined with marble shopping malls.

"What're all those screens?" I asked, trying to change the subject and give the squirming cephalopod a break. "They look like drive-ins."

Houston zoomed his receptors. "Billboards," he confirmed.

"And those big containers on stilts?" Octo asked. "They look a bit too much like water towers for my liking."

"I'll steer clear of them, big guy," I said, gaining altitude as we reached the shoreline. I soared over the forest of water towers and the electric billboards advertising different versions of NED's slow-motion trenchcoats, glow-in-the-dark jackets, designer sunglasses and fancy goblets.

As far as I could see, stretching to the horizon under a cloudless blue sky, were a million more towers, a million more flashing billboards, and millions upon millions of low-rise white shopping centers.

And yet no sign of a single, solitary NED.

"Where is everybody?" I wondered aloud.

"Over there, maybe . . . ?" Octo said, his blue-and-yellow striped tentacle stretching into the cockpit and pointing to the horizon.

Above the skyline, in the distance, something floated. Something just as huge, I figured, as the magma-sucking tanker back on Earth. But it wasn't a spaceship. It looked like hundreds of cathedrals jammed together, painted white, then somehow suspended in mid-air. Beaming from the vast, transparent dome at the summit was a light I would have recognized anywhere in the universe.

It was the unmistakable, ethereal blue glow of Juliet.

CHAPTER THIRTY-EIGHT

Pairing Crashers

I flew towards the mega-cathedral and noticed that the streets below were empty. A NED-Icon royal wedding was clearly the social occasion of the millennium and a must-attend event in the NED world. I figured the NEDs piloting the magma-sucking isosceles hovering above Earth had been at the bottom of the guest list. Everyone else had to be inside the mega-cathedral for the happy day, or glued to whatever passed for television here.

Even as the racer – with its loud fusion engines – touched down on the marble platform surrounding the summit-dome, and even as the four of us strolled beneath the imposing, crystal-arched entrance (beneath which Houston pointed out a pink, shark-shaped Aristox cruiser, parked and silent), we didn't see a soul.

I guess deities just don't worry too much about security.

From inside, we heard music – really beautiful, eerie singing and percussion – and occasional bursts of stadium-volume applause.

"Are we sure this is the right place?" Jessica hissed.

Houston was zoned out, his head tilted as his listened to the music. "Pure perfection," he said.

"Huh?" said Octo.

"That is the sound of Sonya's Balleropera," Houston explained.

I led us inside – cringing as every footstep and whisper echoed around a curved marble corridor with high, arched ceilings – until we finally found a type of backstage area that looked out onto a glass stage. There, Sonya and her two sisters danced for their lives.

In the vast stadium-like structure, millions of NED spectators looked down on the official wedding guests. Thousands of glowing, blue, sparkly-haired Icons on one side, thousands of designer-clothed, mannequin-faced NEDs on the other; all transfixed by the Aristox tribute dance.

And then I saw her.

Juliet sat on a floating throne beside NED. They hovered between the stage and the audience, flanked by their parents. Juliet looked stunning in a sleek, kimono-style dress with her hair pinned up. But she also looked sad, and her glow seemed faded.

NED wore a cheesy pale-blue tuxedo with no hint of irony, and smiled smugly as he focused on the dance ritual, no doubt waiting for Sonya to trip up. He sipped a glowing orange liquid from a crystal goblet and licked his lips with satisfaction. His mother and father looked plump and pleased with themselves, clad in matching, slow-motion flowing robes and plastic hair (had to be genetic), and wearing rage-inducing smirks. Their kid was marrying up.

Juliet's parents, however, looked stern and distant in their ice-blue glow; I guessed this was a well-worn look of utter superiority. Her dad was thin and gaunt, wearing an understated, tight-fitting gray robe, while her mom had a severe bob cut and wore a sparkling white-diamond dress that could have been her attempt to upstage the bride.

Below the floating Pairing party, I spotted the Mentor, who was still in the guise of my mom. She was a weeping mess, blowing her nose through a small forest's worth of tissues. I wasn't sure if she was happy or sad, but either way, her role of Appointed Mentor was about to come to an end.

The entire cathedral was focused on the stage; on

the trio of pink lizards performing their life-risking Balleropera.

Now, dance has never been my entertainment of choice. And dancing plus singing equals musical, and well, that would normally make me think of Jessica – which is never a good thing – but this was different.

This was magical.

Sonya and her sisters, in black, flowing tunics, soared across the stage, immune to gravity. They became each pose, like ever-transforming sculptures, and sang with heavenly voices. Every step and kick and spin got its own harmonies and sometimes chimes too, from little cymbals on their wrists.

It was mesmerizing, even for a musical-hater like me.

The four of us stared from the wings. Octo grinned from all three beaks, tapping his twenty tentacles to the beat. Jessica swayed, entranced, twisting her hair round her fingers like she did when she was a little kid. And Houston was dancing with tiny gestures, matching Sonya's performance move for move. He couldn't take his eyes off her. He was clearly gaga for our favorite pink lizard and if his face wasn't made of metal, I was pretty sure he'd be drooling.

Sonya held an impossible mid-air swan pose and Houston burst into applause. She glanced towards the tinny clapping and, with her concentration broken, lost her grip on the polished glass floor.

SMASH!

Sonya collapsed to the ground, wrist-cymbals crashing and clattering.

One massive intake of breath from the congregation seemed to suck the air out of the cathedral, although Sonya's sisters desperately kept dancing, gaping up at NED with their eyes wide in fear.

"CEASE THE BALLEROPERA!" he yelled, hurling his goblet at the dancers, who scattered to dodge the steaming lava spattering across the stage. "Her misstep has insulted the ritual and I order their punishment!"

The crowd chattered with excitement and my heart lurched as I realized it wasn't the Pairing the NEDs were here to see, it was the chance to catch a lynching.

Sonya hugged her two younger sisters protectively. They looked so frightened and defenseless in front of a million bloodthirsty NEDs.

I had to do something. Without thinking, I ran onto the stage, putting myself between the pink lizards and the red-hot congregation. "Not going to happen, NED!"

The stadium fell silent. All eyes were on me.

"Sherman!" Juliet gasped from above. "What are you doing here?"

"Who dares interrupt this Pairing?" NED's dad bellowed, scowling.

"*Sher*-man," seethed NED.

"Get out of here," I whispered to Sonya and her sisters. "While you can."

Sonya pulled her sisters backstage as NED shouted, "Seize them!"

But Juliet held up a blue hand to silence her partner-to-be. "I want to hear what he has to say."

I pulled the popcorn from my backpack. "Popcorn!" I announced, holding a half-empty box above my head. *Half-empty?* I turned to Octo accusingly.

I was hungry, he mouthed from backstage.

"Popcorn!" I repeated to Juliet. "The most potent symbol of love on my planet. Did my heart love 'til now?"

The congregation gasped.

"What pathetic and desperate plea is this?" mocked NED.

"Do not tempt a desperate man!" I said.

Weirdly, despite a zillion gods watching, I felt none of the fear that had consumed me on Earth when trying to ask Juliet to the movie, and then to the Prom. Here, with certain death looming, and Earth's existence hanging in the balance, I was channeling Romeo – my way of telling her how I really felt, even though (spoiler alert!), Romeo dies at the end.

"Juliet, I've been hiding my real feelings for you behind a plan, and yes, I want to save the Earth, but what good is saving it if I can't be with you? I think you're wonderful, sweet, funny, curious and beautiful, and I should have just told you that from the start instead of waiting for NEDageddon. But I'm telling you now and I think if you Pair with NED, you'll be really unhappy. He only wants you to get himself a seat at the galactic cool table. Yes, I did hope you could stop my planet from being destroyed, but the more I got to know you, the more I fell for you. Yes, I think humanity is worth saving, but I think you and I are worth saving too."

"You're a very good actor," said Juliet.

"I'm not acting. I never was. Do you know why I was suddenly so good at something I used to be so bad at? Because onstage, with you, I wasn't acting. I was just being myself – well, myself in really complicated iambic pentameter and surprisingly comfortable tights, but yes, myself. A star-crossed Sherman who's totally in love with you, my bright angel. Juliet, will you come back to Earth with me as my Prom date? Yes, it's true, I'd hoped that while we're there, you'd be able to stop the NED tanker – but that's not the real reason I'm so into you."

There. I'd said it. I'd put my heart on my sleeve. Now all I could do was wait for Juliet to say yes, float down into my arms, and for us to zoom back to Earth to save the world and dance the night away.

But Juliet had other ideas.

"No, Sherman," she said. "I'm not your trophy, and I'm not your bodyguard."

What? Shakespeare hadn't prepared me for *this*.

CHAPTER THIRTY-NINE

Escape Plan

I was standing, frozen, when Octo slithered onto stage and put a supportive tentacle around me.

"Give us a hug, bro," he said. "I'm really sorry, 'bout everything."

Houston and Jess joined in for moral support. If this was the end, I was glad I was with friends, and though I'd never freely admit it, my sister.

But I wasn't going down without a fight.

"Juliet, you can't Pair with NED!" I said, urging her to see the light. "He's such a . . . *NED!*"

"You're right, Sherman," she said. She stood on her floating throne and addressed the entire cathedral. "I will not be Paired today! Not to NED, not to anyone!"

The congregation gasped again, sucking so much air out of the chamber that I was worried I might faint. The spectators were in an uproar over this breach in decorum.

"Icons have never respected us . . . " I heard someone gossip.

" . . . who does she think she is?"

" . . . does that mean he's on the market again?"

But the pandemonium in the cheap seats was nothing compared to the ferocity on the faces of the Pairing party. I couldn't tell who looked angrier, NED's plump parents or Juliet's furious folks. They started yelling at each other as NED fumed in his throne. He reached out for Juliet's hand but she jumped off her floating chair and drifted down in front of me.

"Thank you, Sherman," she whispered.

"Um, for what? Ruining your Pairing day?"

"No," she said, "for showing me how to be brave enough to break the rules."

Juliet's mother called down to her. "Get back up here, young lady," she commanded, "and complete your journey to Icon."

"I'm sorry, Mother, but I just don't love NED."

"Do you think I love your father?!" her mom shot back.

Octo leaned into me. "Ooh, awkward," he said.

Juliet's father's stern eyes hardened as he looked at her.

"Offspring, you are embarrassing me," he said. "Just say 'I do' and get on with it. It's your path in the universe."

"No, Dad," Juliet said. "He's not for me." She pointed a glowing blue finger at me. "He is."

Juliet's father reached out his hands to his daughter. I thought he was going to lovingly embrace her and tell her that he'd fully support her decision. But he was way worse than my dad. He pulled at the air and suddenly Juliet's glorious blue glow was ripped away, leaving her in mortal, teenage-girl form. She was just as beautiful as before, but now, I realized, just as vulnerable as I was.

"Then you are disowned for this treachery," he said, "and stripped of your immortality!"

Juliet shuddered, looking shocked, but only for a moment. Instead of crying, she smiled. She relaxed her shoulders and her frown disappeared.

"SEEEEEIZE THEM!" yelled NED.

Twenty thuggish-looking NEDs suddenly flew – yep, flew – straight at us from the cathedral floor.

"Please tell me you came with an escape plan?" Juliet asked me, grabbing my hand.

Her hand felt warm, human. I gently squeezed it, checking that she was really there. "I actually hadn't thought beyond the part where I confess my love for you and you jump into my arms."

"Run!" called Jess.

"She's smart, your sister," said Juliet.

"Don't you start," I said.

With both sets of parents yelling at each other, NED throwing a tantrum and the whole congregation in a deafening uproar, the five of us made a break for it.

We dashed backstage and retraced our steps through the outer corridor, but Jessica, Juliet and I struggled to keep up with the gyroscoping ventitent and sprinting robot.

A jagged, crackling bolt of lightning-style energy flashed from behind us. It missed frying us, striking the marble floor instead. But more bolts of lightning shot out, and bits of the roof plummeted and smashed into a million razor-sharp shards. I didn't dare look back. We somehow made it back through the entrance arch and were suddenly bathed in daylight, skidding on megamarble, dodging lightning blasts until we reached the racer. We desperately clambered in. I hoped Carol was strong enough to hold up against the lightning.

Juliet had paused on the ground, looking back at the mega-cathedral, at the life she was forgoing. I couldn't fathom everything she was giving up.

"You could go back and say you're sorry," I said from the cockpit.

"I'm not sorry," she said.

"Good," I said. "Then climb aboard and close that back hatch!"

I fired up the racer's fusion reactors, just as the first NED-thug – green eyes glaring, cape and white hair rippling in the wind – burst from the arch.

Followed by another.

And another.

And another.

All of them aiming silver, pistol-style ray guns at us.

I checked everyone was strapped in, then slammed the accelerator and soared skyward. But the thugs flew straight after us, fast as fighter jets.

"Okay, buddy," Octo called. "Just shake off these maniacs and follow Houston's outlined trajectory back to the wormhole."

I glanced down at the dome, and saw the last of the NED-thugs burst out the entrance and join the swarm, shooting their lightning bolts like they were raging thunderstorms meant just for us; chasing us from their sky.

I could retreat, but to where? Earth was bound to be on the verge of destruction as soon as we made it back through the wormhole highway.

Wormhole.

It suddenly hit me.

A wormhole takes something from one place and instantly transports it to another. It was a cosmic sleight of hand, and if it could transport a spaceship, then why not something much, much bigger? I realized I didn't need an omnipotent bodyguard to save the Earth. I just needed my brain and my friends.

The NED tanker straw was going to suck the magma out of the Earth's core, but if I could slip the straw into a wormhole conduit, I could instantly shift it somewhere else. Somewhere else like right here. I could trick that straw into sucking the magma out of Planet NED!

"Change of plan, Houston," I announced. "Can you find us a spot on this planet to open a wormhole large enough to insert a magma-sucking straw? And Octo, give me your phone, I'm going to call my dad."

The entire racer suddenly shook as tendrils of electricity writhed around the steering column and between my fingers.

"Are we hit?" I yelled. "Guys, are we hit?!"

I wrenched myself round and faced a scowling Jessica. Smoke wisped from the cuffs of her prom dress, and her hair stood perfectly on end.

"What do you think, genius?" she groaned.

"We won't survive another blast like that," said Houston.

"No choice, Romeo," Octo yelled. "You gotta try and lose them in the city. We'll get shot to shrapnel up here, and we ain't reaching orbit anytime soon."

I zipped Carol back towards the maze of malls and, for a few precious moments, thousands of NEDs just watched us fly by with dopey, confused expressions on their faces. Then the whole crowd pulled themselves together and turned after us like a swarm of designer wasps.

"They're back on our tail, space cadets," Octo growled. "Who knew they could fly here?"

"Octo," I yelled. "I have to call my dad!"

"Not on my phone, you won't," he snapped.

"Why not?"

"Two words: roaming and charges. Hank and Urta make me pay my own bill."

"If we live through this," I said, "and we, y'know, save the world and everything, I'm pretty sure NATO will cover our expenses."

With the NED swarm still desperately trying to zap us from between megamarble malls, billboards and water towers, Octo reluctantly passed over his phone and I called my dad.

"Please hang up and try your call again," said the calm, pre-recorded voice of doom.

"You gotta put in the planet code first, Sherman," Octo explained.

"What is it?" shouted Houston and Jessica in stereo.

"Forty-two!"

I punched it in and dialled again.

"Please hang up and try your call again," the voice parroted.

Octo sighed. "You don't do a lot of interplanetary dialling, do you? It's zero-zero-four-two, then wait for the dial tone, then punch in the number," he explained in a sing-song voice, as if I should know it already. I punched in the numbers carefully, hoping that the third time was the charm.

Ring-ring-ring.

"General— I mean, Stationery Officer Capote here."

"Dad, it's me. I really need your help."

"Sherman, where are you? Where's your sister?" Dad asked. I put him on speakerphone so I could keep two hands on the wheel as I swerved and bobbed to avoid death by alien-induced lightning. Safety first.

"Dad, she's with me, and we're on another planet – the NED world. Listen, I don't have time to explain, but the attack I was trying to warn you about is happening now—"

"I should have believed you, son. That ship is drilling

a huge hole in the Earth right by the base, and lowering a massive tube towards it. We've tried to attack the spacecraft, but it's impenetrable by our weapons."

"Of course you should have believed me," I said, "but that tube is actually a straw, a giant straw to suck out the magma from the Earth's core."

"Oh, Sherman, what—"

"Dad, I have a plan, but I need you with me. I need you to help me save the world."

"I'm with you, Sherman. All the way."

"Get back to my jail cell and grab the wormhole conduit."

"The what?"

"The purple bracelet that Octo gave me. You know, the weird guy-to-guy present, and—"

"Whoa," said Octo. "You humans don't have friendship bracelets?"

"Take it to that hole in the Earth," I continued, "and stretch it around the opening before that tube goes in. It will create a vortex – a wormhole that'll instantly send the tube here."

"Top-gun, son. I'm on it. I'll keep the line open to—"

"Um, Mr Capote," interrupted Octo. "That'll be really expensive."

"I'll pay you back!" Dad said.

I weaved and darted through the labyrinth of shopping plazas. The NED swarm followed us, though I was doing my best to shake them. Unsuccessfully. I broke free of the city limits and soared over a white sand desert, gunning for speed. Then we came to a rocky terrain of cliffs and canyons, like the Grand Canyon back home. I was thankful I'd practiced steering the racer through such tight crevices.

The NEDs tried to keep pace, but I was at last able to put some distance between us as I zigged, zagged and zoomed through the maze of canyons and gorges. It took nearly twenty minutes of intense flying, with more than a few complaints from the cabin, but I finally managed to lose the swarm in the rugged outback.

"Up ahead, Sherman," said Houston. "There's a large open area, big enough to stretch the wormhole conduit."

"Dad, are you ready on your side?"

"Standing by, Sherman! We're opening the bracelet around the hole now."

I knew we needed to quickly stretch our bracelet to be big enough to capture the full diameter of the straw.

"Octo," I called. "If we hold onto one side of the bracelet from the racer, can you jump out and hold it steady on the other?"

"I'm your man!"

He teased open the rubber bracelet wide enough to give Jess, Houston and Juliet a good hold of it. "Don't let go, you kids," he said.

Then Octo opened the back hatch, ready to hop out with the bracelet, just as I cleared the warren of canyons and jagged mini-mountains and emerged into the open space that Houston had identified. But there was a reason it was a wide-open space.

"Um, is that a *lake*, buckaroo?"

CHAPTER FORTY

Sacrifice

We emerged above a large blue lake nestled inside a rocky ridge. It was almost a perfect circle, and I remembered learning in Planetology that circular lakes were usually meteor-made. But whatever the origin of the lake, it was still filled with water – a potentially lethal allergen to my best friend.

"Octo," I said. "You can't go in there, it could kill you!"

But the ventitent was on a mission, even if it was a suicide one. "Gonna have to take that risk," he said, pointing a few tentacles to the rocky hills on the horizon. A swarm of NEDs crested the ridge.

They'd found us.

"I'll go," offered Juliet.

Octo shook his head. "Adios, dudes," he bellowed, holding his end of the warp conduit between two tentacles as he dived out. "It was nice knowing yaaaaaaa."

"Octo, no," I cried. "It'll—"

But it was too late.

He splashed down into the water, all twenty tentacles flailing as steam rose from his flailing body. He screamed and shouted a variety of swear words, adding to my GalLang cursing vocabulary, but to his credit, he never once let go of the ever-expanding bracelet.

And neither did the team on the racer. "If he survives," Jess announced, "I am *so* going to be his girlfriend."

I skimmed over the water, stretching open the red conduit until it covered the entire lake, and hovered over the opposite shore.

"That should be big enough," I said. "Let go!"

Our edge of the massive rubber ring fell from the back hatch and settled into shape: a gigantic circle resting on the lake that opened a vortex through time and space.

"Dad, we're in position!"

"Top-gun, Sherman! We've created the vortex on our side, right over the hole the ship made. They're none the wiser and are lowering that giant straw straight down into it!"

Suddenly, the NED world shook and rumbled. The rocky outposts overlooking the lake shuddered, cracked and fell.

The swarming NEDs started to fall out of the sky.

They fell into the water, doggy paddling to stay afloat while the vortex beneath them robbed their planet of its magma.

I turned Carol around and went back for Octo, hoping my friend was still alive.

Instead of dodging laser flashes, I was suddenly dodging hundreds of tumbling, complaining NEDs, all wearing the same bewildered, how-could-this-happen-to-someone-as-awesome-as-me expression as they sploshed in their round lake.

"The magma's the source of their power," I realized. "The straw is draining their planet, sucking the magma into the tanker and taking their strength with it."

I circled the area where Octo had jumped and stared at the water. Finally I saw him surface.

"AAAAAAAAAAAAAAAAAAAAHHHHHHH HHHHHHHHHHHHHHHCHOOOOOOOOOOOO OOOOOOOOO!!!"

It wasn't a sneeze.

It was Sneeze-zilla.

Sneeze-point-eight on the Richter scale.

The kind of sneeze that could burst only from someone staggeringly, alarmingly . . .

Allergic.

The ventitent surfaced amongst three NEDs trying

to use each other as life rafts, but they instantly backed off, swimming away like they were scared of catching something contagious.

Octo's rectangular eyes bulged. His blue-and-yellow striped skin was blackened and charred.

"Oh no," Jessica groaned. "He's hurt bad."

I lowered the racer, hovering just over the lapping water. Houston, Jessica and Juliet each grabbed a couple of tentacles and hauled Octo aboard.

"How is he?" I yelled from the cockpit.

"He's alive, Sherman," said Juliet, "but in bad shape."

"That totally SUCKED," Octo wheezed in a scratchy voice.

"But you did it, buckaroo," I said, turning around and smiling at my flambéed friend. "We'll get you your allergy cream and you'll be Ikea colors once again!"

"Your bravery will go down in history," Houston added, tapping his photo-receptors. "And I got it all on video. It'll go viral."

"And I hope you ventitents heal quickly," Jessica said, checking her watch, "because there's still plenty of Prom left – and I'm in the mood for dancing."

"Feelin' better already," Octo beamed.

"Sherman?" called my dad through the speakerphone. "Did it work?"

"You did it, Dad," I replied. "The conduit's sent that straw through the wormhole all the way here. The Earth is safe, the NEDs are powerless and we're coming home in time for the last bit of Prom!"

I flashed the boosters and prepared to take us back to the wormhole highway.

"No, Sherman, you did it," Dad said. "And I'm so incredibly proud of you."

I don't think he'd ever used the P word with me. It felt good – really good – for about an instant.

"But son," he continued.

With Dad there was always a "but".

"You have a choice to make now," he said, gravely.

"What choice?" I asked.

"If you keep the wormhole open, the NED world will implode . . . and die. At our hands."

He was right. If the straw sucked out the planet's core, the NED world would collapse in on itself just like they'd planned for Earth.

"You, Sherman Capote," Juliet said, "have the power to save their home."

I'd saved our world, but endangered another. And as much I despised NED and his entitled, cruel, uppity planet, was I really ready to let an entire species die?

CHAPTER FORTY-ONE

NED or Alive

As I flew the racer from the surface of the tremor-shocked NED planet, Dad's voice sounded tinny over the speakerphone.

"It's up to you, son," he said. "I know you'll make the right decision."

"But?" I asked, expecting a caveat.

"No but, not this time."

By now I could barely hear him over the colossal earthquake shaking the planet to pieces.

NED was such a bully, and I hated his species for what they'd done to Houston's world, what they'd tried to do to my home, and their hold over the Aristox. But could I let them all perish?

Part of me wanted to rid the universe of these bullies forever, but another part realized that I would become worse than a bully if I did. I was confused. It was all too much.

"Dad, I don't know what to do," I admitted. "I don't know what to do!"

I felt the weight of the world on my shoulders. Then I realized it was Juliet's hands on my shoulders, gently rubbing them from behind my pilot's chair.

"This is a bit what it feels like to be omnipotent," said Juliet. "Every moment of every day, there are worlds to guard and species to save."

I finally understood why she didn't want to be anyone's bodyguard. She had the weight of the universe on her shoulders *all* the time, and sometimes, she just wanted to be a teenager. It made sense that she was at Groom Lake High; it was the one place in the entire universe she could be herself, and not just an Icon. And I had tried to take that away from her.

"And all you can do is follow your heart," she said.

"Sherman, whatever you decide," Dad said, "whatever happens, I just want you to know – you've done great. I'm proud of you, and your mother would be *so* proud."

I thought about Mom. Once when she was in Afghanistan, she'd been brought a patient who was considered the enemy. She operated on the man, saving his life. She didn't have to, and she didn't get anything in return. She just did it because she believed it was the right thing to do. She followed her heart.

"I don't like these NEDs," I said, "but I can't just let them die."

I was a lover, not a fighter. And I really didn't want to be a killer.

"We're going to collapse our side of the wormhole," I declared. "Octo, that'll collapse the whole thing, right?"

"I'm glad *someone* pays attention," he groaned.

"And what happens to that straw if it's still inside?" I asked.

"It'll get smashed to space-smithereens," Octo said. "A collapsed wormhole crushes anything inside it."

We were approaching the Kármán Line of the NED atmosphere and I had 6DoF in my grasp. We were nearly rid of this NEDforsaken planet, but I banked the racer in the sky and shot us back down towards the lake to sabotage the magma-sucking straw.

"He can't go back in the water," Jessica said. She was right. Octo's swimming days were over, but someone needed to dive in, fetch the bracelet and pull it closed.

"I would volunteer," Houston said, "but I'll sink straight to the bottom. When my parents designed our ecto-suits, they forgot that Earth was seventy per cent water."

"I'll do it," I said, making up my mind. "Houston, you take the controls!"

I climbed out of the cabin as Houston slid into my seat.

"Once I come back up with the bracelet, tow me to the other side of the lake. Octo, will that collapse the wormhole?"

"That'll do it. But, Sherman, as soon as the vortex closes, the hole that's left is going to start spewing magma. You'll be opening a hole that goes all the way down to the planet's core."

"You mean I'll be creating a volcano?"

Octo nodded. "Okay, I guess you pay attention in school too."

"Then I'd better be quick," I said, looking out the back hatch at the water rushing below.

Juliet looked at me. "Sherman, you don't have to—"

I took one big breath and jumped out, splashing into the clear lake below. I was suddenly thankful for the Air Force-compulsory swimming lessons, and dived until I could see the stretched, red rubber bracelet. I grabbed it and kicked my way up. But it was heavier than I'd realized. I kicked and kicked, but I wasn't rising. I could feel my body weaken, oxygen leaving from my lungs. I tugged and kicked and wanted to scream. But the lake's surface was so far above me. I stopped kicking, as it dawned on me that this was the end.

At least I'd saved the Earth. At least I'd told Juliet how I really felt about her. And at least I knew how Dad felt about me.

It was my time. A great light encircled me, as if calling me to swim towards it and leave behind my mortal life. I began kicking again. This was my final destiny, my crossing over to the other side.

But it wasn't just a light. It was a glow.

A very familiar blue glow!

I blinked, and suddenly Juliet was floating before me. She leaned in towards me, pressed her warm lips on mine, and blew fresh air into my mouth and into my lungs. As she pulled back, I noticed we were now in a bubble – an air bubble under the water.

"What? How are you doing this?"

"Just kiss me," she said. And I did. On. The. Lips. And considering it was my first non-stage, underwater kiss on an alien planet, it was amazing. Okay, who am I kidding? All qualifiers aside, it was just . . . *amazing*.

She reached down and grabbed my hand . . . the one still holding onto the bracelet . . . and gently pulled it up. We rose steadily in the water until we surfaced with the bracelet.

"Thank you," I said.

"No, Sherman, thank *you*."

"For what?"

"For showing true compassion when faced with ultimate power. I think the Icons could learn from you."

She pointed to a tall rocky outcrop at the far end of the lake. There, hovering on the rock's top, were Juliet's parents, glowing blue. They nodded and then they vanished.

"Maybe they did learn something?" I said.

"Looks like," she said.

Juliet held onto my weakened body and pulled me up into the rear hatch of the racer. Houston immediately revved the racer towards the middle of the lake and the bracelet shrunk in circumference and then snapped to its normal size, coming to its final resting place in the palm of my hand.

I stared at the red rubber circle. The wormhole between worlds was destroyed and the NED planet was safe from certain ruin, but I was still reliving that amazing kiss.

"It's leaving, Sherman!" Dad cheered through the phone, snapping me out of my daydream. "The straw's retracted and the tanker's leaving orbit. They must be hightailing it back there to replace their own magma!"

"That's great, Dad," I said. "We've closed the wormhole from here and—"

Suddenly, lava spewed into the sky. We watched through Carol's windshields as a fountain of red-hot inner-planet goo sprayed all around us.

"Get us out of here, Houston!" I yelled to the cockpit.

Houston navigated the racer upward, but the escaping lava licked at the racer as it towered up, burning through the metal casing of the starboard engine and, from the sound of it, frying the fusion jet inside.

With only one functioning rocket, Houston limped the racer up and over the rocks, to safety, but the damage was done. As soon as we set down, a few miles from the erupting hole in the planet, we scrambled out to examine it.

"Carol's fried," said Octo. He was right; the racer looked more charred than he did. The entire starboard booster was melting and at least half of the cabin's hull was scorched and fractured. But after everything we'd been though, I wasn't giving up hope.

"We might be able to repair it, fly home with just the one engine—" I began as a blinding flash of lightning struck the racer, blowing it to pieces.

I was floored by the force of the explosion, and for a minute couldn't see anything through the billowing smoke.

"Everyone okay?" asked Octo. "Roll call."

"Here," I managed.

"Just when I thought my dress couldn't get any more ruined," said Jessica.

"Operational," said Houston.

The smoke lifted, and I saw that only Juliet, shielded from the blast by her blue aura, was still standing. "That did tickle a bit," she said.

Fortunately for us mortals, we'd been standing far enough back from the blast. I guessed that had we still been inside the racer, we would have been incinerated. I took my eyes from my friends and surveyed the carnage. There was nothing left of Carol. Not one scrap of metal.

She was gone, just like my mom.

Strangely, I heard laughter – sick, smug laughter – blowing on the wind. I looked up. Standing on a rock tower, cape flowing in slow-motion over his powder-blue tuxedo, the fountain of hot lava spewing behind him, was NED.

He was holding the smoking gun.

Hope, it seemed, had given up on me.

CHAPTER FORTY-TWO

Egg on his Face

NED scowled down at us with his self-satisfied mannequin-face and plastic hair that was perfectly still despite the gale from the spewing lava.

"Perhaps I should talk to him," Juliet sighed. "I know he's mean, but . . . what I did to him, that must have really hurt."

NED pointed his silver ray gun at us, taking aim.

"I think he's way past *talk*," I said.

"Prepare to—" he began, no doubt about to issue the last words he thought we'd ever hear. But I'm pretty sure NED never expected a giant flying egg to knock him off his pedestal.

I gaped in disbelief as he fell backward, tumbling down the rock tower and into a deep crevice. Sonya's Eggcraft swung back around, hovered over us and opened its hatch.

"Hiya, wedding crashers," she said with a smile as she

hung out of the back, still wearing her black Balleropera tunic. "Looks like you could use a lift."

She disappeared inside to set the egg down on terra now-firma, then rushed down the gangplank, busting out some grateful hugs for everyone.

"Octo, you look a little crispy," she said.

"He looks just great to me," chirped Jessica.

"So gross," I said. "Good to see you, Sonya."

"How did you find us?" asked Houston, holding his Sonya-hug the longest.

"I packed my sisters off in the cruiser, but figured you might need a hand with your *NED*festation problem. But then I couldn't find you. It wasn't until I spotted that lava spray that I thought to myself, it could only be the handiwork of someone wanted by NATO for inciting global thermo-nuclear war."

"I'm glad I didn't disappoint," I said.

"C'mon aboard and let's get out of here," she said, stopping to grab my arm. "And, Sherman, thanks for helping me and my sisters."

"No prob," I said. "And thank you, for everything – especially for getting me behind the wheel of a rocket."

I looked over the burning chunks of metal strewn across the rocky landscape. "Goodbye, Carol," I said.

Sonya followed my gaze to the scorched patch of

ground and lowered her head, whispering solemnly, "She reached for the stars."

"And she got there," I said, "in the end."

Jessica put one hand on my shoulder, holding an Octo tentacle with the other. Juliet reached over and squeezed my right palm. The gushing lava painted the sky deep orange as the planet retched its insides out. I felt a little bit like that: my deeper feelings finally coming to the surface.

I couldn't stop the tears. They dripped from my eyes and raced down my face. I could taste the salt. But I wasn't embarrassed. I squeezed Juliet's hand back and nodded a slow, deliberate signal of reconciliation to Jessica.

"Octo?" I asked, using my sleeve as a tissue. "Do you think you could get us back to the wormhole highway to make the end of Prom?"

Octo wrapped a tentacle around Jess and said, "Only if I get a dance."

We piled aboard the Eggcraft and I took the co-pilot seat beside Sonya.

"Wanna fly her?" she asked.

"You bet," I said. I was a rocket man, a rocket-savant, but I'd found my true calling. I was born to fly.

Must be something in the genes, I decided.

I befriended the controls and steered the Eggcraft up into the sky, past the NED Kármán Line, and out of the atmosphere to Octo's coordinates. We found the on-ramp to the wormhole highway, and I took one last look back at Planet NED and smiled. I'd faced down the bullies and refused to become one myself.

CHAPTER FORTY-THREE

Hero's Welcome

Soon after we pushed through Earth's atmosphere, two not-so-friendly F-18s escorted us back to Groom Lake. I set us down back in the scrapyard; a perfect landing lit by the spotlights of the eight armored Humvees that surrounded us. A helicopter whirled directly overhead and the two fighter jets flew past.

"Sherman Capote," barked a megaphone voice. "Leave the spacecraft with your hands in the air."

"*Egg*craft!" corrected Sonya.

"No other occupants are to disembark," ordered Megaphone Man.

It's not like I'd expected a hero's welcome or anything, but a friendly slap on the back for a "job well done" wouldn't have gone amiss. But I guessed that as far as the military were concerned, Sherman Capote was a fugitive who'd committed some serious rocket-related reoffending.

I squeezed from the cockpit into the cabin and grinned as Juliet said, "You're a real hero, whether they recognize it or not."

Sonya opened the hatch and Octo slithered out a tentacle, scooping up the allergy cream from his nearby Toyota.

"Ooooooh, that feels soooo, soooo good," he purred. As he lathered up, the cream erased the chargrilled flesh, revealing raw, shiny blue-and-yellow stripes underneath.

"Only Sherman Capote," barked Megaphone Man again. "With your hands up."

"Don't forget me when I'm gone," I said, heading for the gangplank.

Jessica enveloped me in a hug and punched me on the arm. "You did great, Sherman. Really great."

"It's been a pleasure flying with you, pilot," said Sonya with a smile.

"You made me think I had a brother again," said Houston. "Jessica, you are very lucky."

"I know," she said, smiling at me.

"C'mere, buckaroo," said Octo. He wrapped twenty tentacles around me, pulling me close for a suffocation-inducing hug.

"C-c-can't breathe," I stuttered. He released his grip and slipped the red bracelet around my left wrist.

"A little something for the gulag," he said. "We'll be waiting on the other side."

"Where will that be?" I asked.

"In fair Verona," said Juliet. She took both of my hands, looked me straight in the eyes and kissed me, her lips warm and electric. "Go face them like the hero you are."

I stepped off the ship with my hands up and my eyes squinted against the harsh lights. Four Military Police rushed me and forced me to the ground. I could taste engine oil in the sand and feel the handcuffs cut into my wrists. My heart thumped in rhythm with the beating helicopter blades above.

"UNHAND THAT AIRMAN!"

Dad's voice rang out over the noise and chaos. "I SAID, UNHAND THAT AIRMAN!" he boomed again.

"Stationery Officer, um, sorry, General Capote . . ." stammered one of the men, hoisting me to my feet and unclipping the cuffs. I noticed Dad was wearing his fully decorated general's dress uniform again. I guessed he'd received a promotion in light of the world not being destroyed.

"Sherman just saved this entire planet," he growled, signaling the officers to lower their weapons. "The world's leaders have sent their commendations and all charges have been dropped."

"No gulag?" I asked.

Dad smiled, shook his head and wrapped me in a vice-grip hug. "Not for my son. Not on my watch!"

Jessica was soon sprinting from the ship and all three of us stood there hugging. My family was – at last – a family again. I looked over to the Eggcraft, to my friends, silhouetted at the ship's entrance. The aliens who'd returned home.

"Uh-um," interrupted a female voice behind us, clearing her throat. I turned to see Juliet's Mentor, stepping into the spotlights. "If you've finished your tactile display of affection, I believe these youngsters have a dance to attend. Which I am under Icon orders to chaperone."

Epilogue

Octo was already fully healed by the time we made our grand entrance at Prom.

The gym was packed with dancing students, thrashing to a Taylor Swift cover of the Beastie Boys' 'Intergalactic'. Martian tripods loomed over the dancing masses, lit by flashing lights and disco balls. But as soon as they spotted us, the music stopped, their swaying halted, and the aliens all stood and stared.

Klaatu the Martian stepped forward and slowly clapped his little hands. For what felt like the longest moment, no one else joined in.

Octo whispered to me, "Uh oh, slow-clap fail."

But one by one, the other aliens joined in until the gym shook with applause.

I looked at the sweaty sea of aliens, this cheering student body of thirty-eight species. Just a few weeks ago, they were strangers to me. Now, still strangers to humanity, they were *my* people and I felt like I finally fitted in somewhere.

Juliet reached out her hand and as I looked over, I did a double take – she wasn't blue. She was back in human, teenage-girl form.

Jess held Octo's tentacle, and Sonya took Houston's arm. I looked over at the snack table and caught Dad and the Mentor comparing notes on raising teenagers while choosing which Rilperdough to indulge in. As soon as they bit into their sentient pastries, they both just smiled at us.

We strode to center-court as returning heroes and saviors of the Earth, but mostly as friends. They weren't just the best friends I'd ever had; they were the best friends I could have ever wished for.

And when the DJ put the music back on, David Bowie's 'Space Oddity', we danced like we'd just survived the War of the Worlds.

- The End -

Acknowledgments

This project has been a long-gestating labor of love. I first dreamed up Sherman, Jess and the crazy idea of a high school for aliens while I was on holiday. I became so obsessed with these characters and their world that I felt compelled to put pen to paper (and thus, it wasn't much of a holiday). I have to thank some key people for being part of the journey.

My wife Sidonie for believing in this story and encouraging me to keep going with it.

Matt Knight for helping to bring Sherman's story to life.

Catherine Coe for her editing skills and Emma Young for her fantastic final copy-edits.

George Edgeller and John Bond at whitefox for turning words into reality.

Everyone from Nelson High School in the early 90s for giving me the raw material to draw from. I've never been to a high school for aliens, but I sure did feel like an alien in high school.

And lastly, I want to thank you, the reader. I crafted this story for you, to make you laugh, cry, and maybe think. Everything in life is basically high school; groups of people clustering in cliques trying to get by. And if we're kind to each other, maybe that's the key to peace in the galaxy . . . or at the very least, in the school cafeteria.